MAREK

by

Ralph Palim

The Conrad Press

Marek
Published by The Conrad Press in the United Kingdom 2024
Tel: +44(0)1227 472 874
www.theconradpress.com
info@theconradpress.com
ISBN 978-1-916966-18-5
Copyright © Ralph Palim 2024
All rights reserved.
Typesetting and Cover Design by: Levellers
The Conrad Press logo was designed by Maria Priestley.
Printed and bound in Great Britain by Clays Ltd, Elcograf S.p.A.

Acknowledgements

Towards the end of the Covid-19 lockdown I, like many people, became bored. A possible activity was to write a novel. The subject came to me when I was perusing through *Lost Countries: Tales from an Old Stamp Album* by Stuart Laycock and Chris West. The authors describe the issue of postage stamps by countries which no longer exist. To call them 'countries' is to exaggerate – many were short-lived rebellions which needed stamps just for credibility.

I discovered the story of the Czechoslovak Legion and its stamps, issued during the First World War and the Russian revolution. The stamps were used on the Legion's active postal service.

I am indebted to the authors of two other books:

The Czech and Slovak Legion in Siberia, by Joan McGuire Mohr.

Dreams of a Great Small Nation, by Kevin J. McNamara.

These two books gave me many facts about the Legion and the circumstances in Russia at the time. Without them this book could not have been written.

Introduction

The First World War is the background to the story of the Czechoslovak Legion. The war was started by two absolute rulers, the elderly Habsburg Emperor Franz Joseph and the Russian Tsar Nicholas.

They and their ancestors had ruled their empires for hundreds of years. Life at court isolated them from the lives of their subjects. They were often surrounded by sycophants and interfering relatives who kept them from knowing how the mass of their subjects lived. They received little truthful information about other countries. Advisers frequently gave their leaders the sort of information and advice they thought would please them.

Hubris and arrogance developed in the Tsars of Russia and this is evident in their successors, down to the present day. Their decisions were rash and caused untold misery and deaths among their own people and in neighbouring countries. Millions of illiterate workers on both sides killed each other without any idea why they were doing so. In four years they destroyed each other's four-hundred-dynasties.

Many men of the oppressed minorities in the Austro-Hungarian empire were forced to wear, and died wearing, the hated uniform of the German-speaking elite. Some rebelled in 1914. Some Czechs and Slovaks formed a brigade, the Czechoslovak Legion within the Russian army but responsible to their leaders in France, where many of their countrymen had joined the fight against Germany in a legion within the French army. The Legion increased in numbers when prisoners in Russian prisons were recruited and the Legion grew to be a fully-fledged army of over 100,000 men.

The Legion was an unusual army. The literacy rate among the men was about ninety-eight percent compared to the Russian army where it was about two percent. The Legion became a very effective fighting force.

This book tells a little of their fortunes and misfortunes against the ever changing political and military events in Russia from 1914 to 1920. It is told through the eyes of a fictional character, Marek, and his friends.

Ralph Palim

Marek

Chapter One

Marek was conscious of a severe pain in his left arm. He felt dizzy, half-awake. From his position lying down he became fascinated by a large crack in the ceiling. He looked around. Despite the darkness in the room he began to perceive some features. There were other men lying on beds so he must be in a barrack room. Then he dozed off.

Coming to, a large man in a white coat was standing next to the bed. He spoke quietly in Russian.

'We took out a bullet from your left arm but you had lost a lot of blood. How is your pain?'

'Severe,' replied Marek. 'Morphine,' he requested.

'Sorry I haven't got any. This is a field hospital, we are not in Moscow.'

Despite the pain, Marek fell asleep. He dreamt of his childhood in Moravia, his parents, school and the small home town where he had grown up.

Chapter Two

Marek was born on June 28, 1892. His father, Pavel Novak was a cobbler by trade working in the town of Zlin in Moravia, located within the Habsburg empire of Austria and Hungary. The Emperor, Franz Josef, had the dual titles of Emperor of Austria and King of Hungary. Moravia was only one part of a huge empire of more than fifty million people stretching across much of central and south east Europe. There were Austrians, Hungarians, Czechs, Slovaks, Poles, Ruthenians, Croats, Serbs, Slovenes, Italians, Romanians and Islamic Slavs.

The Zlin area was a region known for producing good quality leather footwear as far back as anyone could trace. For four or five generations Pavel's ancestors had been cobblers.

Pavel had grown to be a tall, muscular youth, handsome in a rugged sort of way, polite but rather reserved and certainly not gregarious. He was not academic but was nevertheless curious about life and how things worked. He had three close friends and apart from playing football they spent many happy days in the nearby mountains, hiking, camping and developing a knowledge and love of the forest.

Soon after his sixteenth birthday Pavel joined the Zlin town *Schützenverein*, the German name for a 'marksmen's club.' Such associations or clubs were common in German - speaking countries, originating hundreds of years ago as town militia, citizens coming together to protect themselves from bandits and cattle thieves. Pavel enjoyed the parades, shooting and the fellowship of other men. In August each year the club organised a festival for the people of the town – food, tea, coffee, beer, games, dancing, children's entertainment. Everyone dressed in the national costume.

At age twenty-one Pavel went to a music festival in a neighbouring town. He had little musical ability but enjoyed listening to choirs. After the concert tea was served and he got into a conversation with a pretty, dark haired girl who had been singing in a visiting ladies choir. They were immediately attracted to each other. Pavel found social conversation difficult. Taciturn by nature, he nevertheless managed to carry on a conversation for a good half hour.

Well, in fact, the girl did most of the talking. She gave her name as Veronika. Her family were owners of a small, high quality glassmaking factory in an area of Bohemia which had gained an international reputation for the design and production of glassware. Their conversation was cut short by the call for the choir to leave for home but at the last moment the young folks managed to exchange addresses.

Veronika told her parents of her meeting with a charming young man at the music festival. They didn't take much notice, blithely assuming that their twenty year old daughter would meet many more admirers before there could be any suggestion of marriage. Over the next two months the youngsters corresponded. Veronika wrote long chatty letters whereas Pavel's were short, commenting on local news, which was scarce. Eventually she suggested to her parents that he make a visit to her home-town when they could meet him. It was quite a long journey by train, involving a change of trains in Prague. Many of the glass making factories in Bohemia were located in the areas bordering Germany and Austria where the majority language was German. However Veronika's family lived and worked in a small town north of Prague. They were among the significant minority of inhabitants who spoke Czech as their mother tongue.

'But you hardly know him,' protested her mother, taken aback by her daughter's suggestion.

'That's true,' replied Veronika, 'but unless I spend time with him I can't get to know him, can I ? I can't go to Zlin so the only alternative is for him to come here.'

Veronika's father doted on his only daughter and wished always to please her. But he didn't want any young man to take her away. Eventually the parents agreed that if Pavel were to visit their town he could come to tea. There was no question of him staying with them. The visit took place and it was not a success. Afterwards Veronika and her parents discussed Pavel.

'He seems a pleasant young man, very limited education,' commented her father. 'Did he say that his people were Protestant?'

'Yes, they are,' confirmed Veronika.

'That settles it! You should not see him again. No son or daughter of mine will marry a Protestant. We are a Roman Catholic family and we will remain so,' he declared..

So there it rested for some months. They continued to correspond, his letters sent to her via a helpful cousin. Then he made several visits to her town, careful not to go near her house.

Finally Veronika decided to have it out with her parents. She appreciated their concern for her. She attended church every Sunday without much enthusiasm but enjoying the music. In fact she didn't much care for the rituals of the Catholic Church.

'All right,' said her father 'but I must speak to him. If there is to be a marriage then it must take place in the Catholic cathedral and you must both promise to bring up your children, if you are blessed with offspring, as devout Catholics. Your mother and I insist on this condition.'

In fact the parents were not at all happy. Their intelligent, well-educated daughter was marrying beneath her station. She would soon get bored with her cobbler husband. But she was clearly determined to go ahead. In a few weeks she would celebrate her twenty- first birthday and from then she could do as she wished. They decided to give in gracefully. Pavel also gave in gracefully to the demand that the wedding be held in a Catholic cathedral. It was a take-it or leave-it choice, so he had really no alternative.

The wedding took place in the cathedral of the nearest city to Veronika's home town. It was followed by a lavish reception which her parents insisted on hosting despite Veronika's wish for a more simple celebration. Finally she gave in to all the arrangements, commenting to Pavel, 'Well, I suppose it will be my mother's big day.' All the family's business associates and local dignitaries had to be invited. She looked splendid in her white gown and he appeared rather uncomfortable in the ill-fitting borrowed suit.

Back in Moravia the new family settled into a routine. Pavel continued to earn sufficient from the small shoe making business which he had taken over on the death of his father. Veronika established the household and then began to work with children in the local school. She started a small choir singing folk songs. The older children were not at first interested but joined in when they saw the success of their younger siblings. After a couple of years Veronika took the children to sing at the annual music festival where she and her husband first met.

Pavel got on well with other cobblers in the town. He had been at school with one friend, Tomas Bata, until they left at age 12 to start their training as cobblers. In 1894 Tomas, his brother Antonin and sister Eva decided to set up a company to make and sell shoes. They borrowed 800 florins from their mother, rented a couple of rooms and began to employ other cobblers. Although Pavel had his own business he often collaborated with Bata and helped him when the new business ran into financial problems.

Leather had become increasingly expensive so that people could not afford the products, so Tomas started making shoes from canvas. Initially Pavel was sceptical of what he regarded as substandard shoes but he had to accept that they were very popular due to the cheap price. Tomas's company expanded, employees were given steady work and a regular wage and other cobblers worked for him from their homes in villages near Zlin.

Five years after the formation of the company Tomas heard of machines developed in America to manufacture shoes, so taking three employees he sailed from Germany to Boston and then travelled on to Lynn, site of a factory making shoes by machine. He and the three employees took jobs doing menial work on the production line where they learned all they could about the machines and the way the production was organised.

After six months they returned home, stopping off in England and Germany. Back in Zlin Tomas introduced machines and techniques which made Bata Shoe Company the first to manufacture mass produced shoes in Europe.

Marek's childhood was similar to that of most boys in his town. School was taught in German so that they all became fluent in that language. Out of school they spoke Czech. Activities included football, camping, hunting, playing chess in the long winter evenings which began about four o'clock, just after school ended. At age sixteen he was very proud to join his father as a member of the *Schützenverein* and to take part in all their activities.

Every summer Veronika took Marek to stay with her parents. They became fond of their grandson and encouraged him to play with his cousins. On every visit they took him to the glass factory where he marvelled at the work of the glass blowers. As he grew older his grandfather explained to him how the business was managed. It was now exporting a wide range of high quality glassware to a dozen countries. Occasionally Marek met foreign buyers, some from as far away as England. They were impressed by the young boy's attempt to speak English.

On these visits, Veronika took him to the Catholic church on Sundays and special Saint's Days. She didn't tell her parents that this was the only time in the year, apart from Christmas and Easter Sunday, when they attended mass.

Marek had a stubborn, adventurist streak to his character, frequently getting himself into trouble. His father Pavel was a quiet rebel, longing for independence for the Czech and Slovak lands. He hated what he regarded as the stranglehold that Vienna held over the people of the Habsburg empire. It was dangerous to express such opinions but Pavel was open about the subject.In long talks with the young Marek, he described the battle of White Mountain in 1620 when Czechs were defeated and many were executed. He described how other revolutions over the centuries were put down ruthlessly by Austrian troops.

Of course from an early age Marek helped his father at his job as a cobbler. He became competent in cutting and sewing leather but not quick at it. He was bored by it. At age fourteen he left school and went to serve his apprenticeship at the expanding Bata Shoe Company, where his father now worked in addition to continuing his own business part-time.

Veronika monitored his school studies and encouraged him in appreciation of music. She continued to tutor him after he left school and even taught him the basics of English which she had learned as a child. He was a quick learner in all subjects and from age sixteen he made up his mind to leave cobbling and seek his fortune in the wider world. That probably meant Prague, where he would study and work for Czech independence.

In 1909, about the time of his seventeenth birthday, Marek told his parents of his wish to study at the University in Prague. Veronika already knew of his intention and indeed had helped him to get the information and application forms to apply for admission. This upset his father. The family had always been cobblers and that was what he wanted his son to continue doing, one day taking over his business.

Pavel decided to speak with his old friend and employer, Tomas Bata about Marek, to whom the boy was still apprenticed. The Bata Shoe Company had grown beyond everyone's expectations. Sadly Antonin Bata, co-founder died in 1908. There were now nearly five hundred full-time workers and many more who worked at home in their cottages in the nearby villages. The company had begun to export its shoes which were manufactured in various attractive styles. A sales agency was opened in Germany and there were plans to expand in other countries.

Tomas was sympathetic towards his old friend Pavel. A few days later he asked Pavel and Marek to meet him at his house. Tomas explained that the business was experiencing growing pains. The administrative procedures, especially concerning the welfare of staff, needed attention. He was experiencing stress himself. There just weren't enough hours in the day. So he asked if Marek would be prepared to come and help him in the office. This could lead in due course to an important position. Tomas recognised Marek's growing self-confidence. No one in the company spoke any English except himself, a language which would become increasingly important.

Tomas observed that Marek didn't jump at this opportunity so he suggested that Pavel talk it over with his son and that they should meet again the following week.

'This is a fantastic opportunity. You could make a great career. It's such a great company. Superb products. And look how they are looking after the workers. There is a clinic, school for the children of employees, and so much more to be done.'

They kept the appointment the following week. Tomas came straight to the point.

'Well, have you thought about my offer'? he asked, addressing the question to Marek.

Marek was silent for what seemed a long time. Finally he spoke, quietly in a way that was not typical of him.

'I know that it is a great opportunity and I have great respect for you and everything that you have achieved. But this is not what I want to do with my life. I want to go to university in Prague and work for the independence of the Czech and Slovak people. That is my goal in life.'

Now it was the turn of Pavel to be speechless. He felt an internal conflict. The job was a unique opportunity. But he was proud of his son's determination to work for independence, dangerous though that work might be. After a long time, he uttered only one sentence.

'Boy, the decision is yours. Whatever you decide I will respect it'

Chapter Three

Veronika insisted on accompanying Marek to Prague in order to 'settle him in.' On arrival they immediately went house hunting. Well, they looked for a student room.

'We have to look in the Old Town,' insisted Marek. 'It is near the university and where many of the students live.'

They looked at half a dozen rooms but none appeared attractive. Then Veronika noticed a sign on the second floor of an old building saying 'Student room to let.' She knocked on the door and an elderly man opened it.

'I see that you have a room to let. My son is looking for a room. Could you show it to us?'

'Certainly. Please come in. I will call my wife and she can show it to you.'

His wife appeared and led them upstairs. The room was rather small but tastefully furnished and there was a bathroom. She said that he could invite in visitors during the day but she insisted that noisy parties were not permitted.

'Do you have to practice on a musical instrument,' she enquired. 'My husband and I like to have a quiet house, especially in the evenings.'

'No, I am not studying music and I will not bring an instrument here,' Marek confirmed to her.

The rent she quoted seemed reasonable so they agreed to take it. The lady asked for the first week's rent before she handed over the keys. After a few more explanations they thanked her and left.

Marek concluded, 'If I don't like it I can move. When I get to know some other students they will advise me if I want to find somewhere else.'

They went on to enrol in the university. That done, they spent a couple of days sightseeing, Marek making a mental note of the places he would like to return to.

The Charles University in Prague was one of the oldest and most prestigious in Europe. For many years it had been divided into two sections. For more than a hundred years there had been stressful rivalry between them. At the time that Marek enrolled the two separate institutions were the German Charles - Ferdinand University and the Czech Charles – Ferdinand University. The former had several eminent people associated with it including the scientist Albert Einstein and the writer Franz Kafka. It had a library of more than 25,000 books.

The Czech University was not so well known internationally but did have a history of learned teachers, including Professor Tomas Masaryk, who taught there in the last twenty years of the nineteenth century. In the University and in the public square he had a profound impact on the peoples' understanding and appreciation of Czech culture and heritage.

Marek enrolled in the Czech University and joined the 2,500 students. Although he was fluent in German and actually wrote the language more easily than Czech, he disliked it as the language of his oppressors. He registered for courses covering law, economics, government, military history, English, and Czech art, culture and music.

Professor Masaryk gave a visiting lecture at the University in 1911. He had held the position of Professor of Philosophy many years before his visit. He spoke enthusiastically about his passion, Czech culture and the need for devolution of many sections of government to the Czech people, all within the overall structure of the Habsburg Empire. After the lecture he shook hands with many of the students. Marek took the opportunity to tell the eminent professor that he was wrong about devolution of powers.

'That old fool Emperor Franz Josef and his stupid advisers will never agree. If we want independence, one day we will have to fight for it.'

'I hope that it will never come to that,' the Professor replied. Marek had the impression that the reply was expressed more in hope than conviction.

At the end of the first year, Marek went home to his parents and then made a visit to his grandparents, staying for almost a month. Employees were taking their annual one week vacation in turn, so Marek was able to take over some of their duties. He was kept a safe distance from the production area, but he helped with the stores, moving, counting and recording items manufactured, then packaging for shipment.

Marek quickly learnt the book-keeping procedures – recording sales, purchases of materials and wages, the cash payments including amounts drawn by his grandfather for personal and family expenses. The old boy insisted on keeping the Private Ledger, which brought together the totals of the activities and which would show the annual profit. He kept it in the safe in his office and didn't allow anyone else to see it.

Towards the end of the stay his cousins returned. Jan was twenty-five years old and it was an open secret that he was being groomed to take over the running of the business. His grandfather was in his early sixties and his health was deteriorating so he needed to bring in a family member to ensure that the glassworks remained in the family. At one long dinner, followed by more beer, Marek and Jan talked about glassmaking.

'Glassmaking is a very old industry, going back to Roman times. So after that there are records of glass being made in Bohemia. As you know, Bohemian glass is now famous throughout Europe and America for the quality of the glass and the imaginative designs.'

'How did you acquire such a wide knowledge of the subject?' enquired Marek.

'I grew up in the town so I remember the factory since I was five years old and as a young teenager I earned some pocket money doing odd jobs there just as you have been doing. Then when I was seventeen grandad paid for me to go to the glassmaking school, Kamenicky Serov. The professors were very knowledgeable about the processes of glass making.'

'Many years ago our ancestors learnt how to combine sand, silica, soda and potash under a high temperature to make glass. Then if lead oxide is added you get crystal. This is softer and easier to cut and shape.'

There was a lot to learn and I still try to keep up with developments. I have just come back from a seminar in Prague on design. Very interesting. The speakers stressed the importance of studying nature – not only from books but by walking in the countryside, really looking at flowers and leaves to appreciate their beauty. Our best designer is a lady. She joined us after studying art in Prague.'

'Why does the factory specialise in drinking glasses and vases?' asked Marek.

'Well, there are so many things we could do, but we obviously can't do all of them. Jewellery, for example. We have tried it and may well decide to expand. Chandeliers have been made in Bohemia for many years. In fact, Bohemian chandeliers hang in the great palaces of Europe, Vienna, Versailles, St Petersburg. There is too much competition from larger well established companies for us to get into that market. But we can and will expand.'

'Jan, there is something troubling me. I am not sure whether I should say this, so please regard it as confidential.'

'Go ahead,' replied Jan with a puzzled look on his face.

'In the last two weeks I have prepared a lot of summaries of sales and costs which I have given to Grandad. He puts all these totals into the Private Ledger which he keeps in his office. Presumably he works out the profit. I can't do so but I have noted that the total of the expenses is almost as high as the sales. The difference is far less than the drawings, that is the money that he takes out for the family's living costs. If that is so, I don't know how the business can survive in the long run unless costs are brought down, not to speak of money needed to expand the factory.'

There was a long silence. 'What you say, if you are correct, is very worrying. I will do some research myself. Anyway, thank you for telling me this. Be assured that it will remain confidential.

They retired to bed. Jan did not sleep soundly, waking several times to think about what Marek had told him.

The first two years in Prague passed very pleasantly. It was easy to make friends among other students, nearly all men. In the old town there was a balanced mixture of sexes. Despite taking his studies seriously Marek found time for other activities. Concerts, operas and ballet performances could be attended for a small price sitting up in the 'gods.'

The music was superb. Recent work by Czech composers, Leon Janacek and the late Antonin Dvorak, as well as the Hungarians, Bela Bartok and Franz Liszt were favourites of the Prague audiences. Italian opera was at its height, Giacomo Puccini following on the superb works by Giuseppe Verdi. Marek returned several times to enjoy the works of an Austrian composer, the Jew

Gustav Mahler, particularly his symphonies and 'Das Lied von der Erde,' that despairing yet blissful hymn to earthly life.

Marek joined the army cadets, not out of any sense of loyalty to the Habsburg empire: on the contrary, he had a vague notion that war – perhaps civil war – would occur in the next decade. Training was limited to learning how to handle a rifle, including a few visits to a rifle range, and marching on parades as well as talks encouraging cadets to enlist in the army.

The meetings gave the cadets plenty of exercise so that Marek kept physically fit. He enjoyed the games of football and the rather riotous parties after the meetings. After six months he became bored with the sessions so after the vacation he allowed his membership to lapse.

Marek kept up to date with national and world affairs, which he had followed as a boy. The newspapers were full of reports of events in Serbia ever since the Turks had been driven out. A king was installed and then assassinated in 1903. His successor became effectively a prisoner of the group which had installed him. Attempted coups and arrests continued over the next decade. The Serbian people longed for the union of all Serbs and independence from Austria. Opposition to the rule by Emperor Franz Josef was growing across the Habsburg empire.

The British Empire was at its height and Germany was challenging its military supremacy. Russia also was rearming after its disastrous defeat by Japan in 1905. In China the Emperor had been deposed and a republic was declared. Several factions competed for power and a long civil war began.

It was in his third year in Prague, returning from the Christmas break, that Marek met Maria. They sat next to each other at a concert, got talking and afterwards went for a drink. Dark, pretty, vivacious, she told Marek that she was in her last year at the conservatory learning to play the violin. They agreed to meet again. The ball season began, that hectic time of merry-making before lent. So Marek and Maria attended as many balls as they could and their friendship developed.

Maria was very well informed about the musical life of the city. She was familiar with the major works for violin and was quite critical of the local performances. Marek gradually noted that she could be quite cynical and ironic but always amusing.

In late March, Maria explained that she would have to visit Vienna. She had been in touch with a famous violin teacher and she wished to continue her studies with him. He could see her on the Thursday following Easter.

'Why don't we go together?' she proposed. Marek had heard so much about Vienna but he had never been there and he admitted to himself that he was getting very fond of Maria. The timing was ideal. He would spend the first week of the vacation, including Easter Sunday back home with the family. The following day he would return early to Prague.

'That would be great. I would love to go with you and we should have a wonderful time in Vienna.'

'I'll get the rail tickets and arrange somewhere for us to stay that is not too expensive,' Maria said.

So at mid-day on the Monday after Easter they boarded the express for Vienna, travelling second class. The train passed through beautiful countryside and in just over four hours they arrived in Vienna. Maria had been to Vienna several times as a child with her parents and knew the city quite well. She quickly found the right turn to the third district and the house where they would stay.

The doorbell was answered by a rather grumpy old lady who explained a few house rules. She then showed them to their room on the second floor. Marek was taken aback by the thought of sharing a room but he accepted the arrangement without discussion. In fact, he was rather excited by it.

'Well, two rooms for a week would have been too expensive,' Maria explained. This was not true - the rent was calculated per person and Maria knew it!

After a long walk they returned to their room and getting into the large bed, Marek wondered what would now happen. Maria knew! She took the initiative and they made love, making sure that she would not become pregnant. Marek was certain that he was not the first man Maria had slept with.

The architecture of Vienna was impressive. The Ringstrasse was a short distance from their room so Marek and Maria walked a good part of it on their first full day. They soon reached the State Opera House, then past the Parliament building opposite to the Hofburg, then on their left the new Rathaus, or city hall. These buildings were all designed to impress and they did so. One day they found their way to Schönbrunn, the royal palace in the countryside just outside the city. On another day, or rather evening, they sat in the vineyards at Grinzing, the village on the outskirts of the city where wine was grown. They had no time for a sail on the 'Blue Danube' river. In fact, it appeared to be a rather murky grey in colour. Disappointing, even though the busy river traffic was interesting.

No less impressive than the buildings was the cultural renaissance of Vienna. The city was one of three or four major centres in Europe for the development of medicine and probably the leader in psychiatry, Sigmund Freud being known worldwide for his developments in the field.

Vienna had always been the European centre of musical composition and performance since the days of Mozart, von Beethoven, Schubert and more recently Bruckner and Mahler, to name a few. New, more experimental compositions were being developed – which were not unanimously welcomed.

In the fields of art new styles were appearing, influenced by the Art Nouveau movement. The artist Gustav Klimt produced erotic paintings such as 'The Kiss,' featuring a couple elaborately robed, to which the artist added gold and silver leaf. His work was not popular with everyone, some describing it as pornographic. Authors broke new ground with novels and poetry. All this was stimulating for Marek even though he somehow rejected the splendour of the buildings. To him, they blatantly projected the power of the Habsburg dynasty.

They explored Vienna by day and attended concerts in the evening. They made two visits to the Musikverein but the highlight was a performance of Tosca at the State Opera. Prague had nothing to compare with the building. Maria's audition with the great man went well and she was offered a place provided that she completed her present studies satisfactorily.

The days and nights passed happily. However, Marek was concerned that he began to feel upset by some of Maria's attitudes and comments. One afternoon on the day before they left for Prague they reached the Jewish quarter on a walk. Maria made some derisive comments which shocked Marek. A discussion followed between them in which Maria expressed strong antisemitic ideas. Marek tried to bring some balance into the discussion, with mention of the contributions to music by Mendelssohn, Mahler and other Jews. Such antisemitic sentiments were not unusual in central Europe but to hear them expressed so vehemently by an educated, cultured person like Maria really upset him.

Back in Prague, they agreed to meet on the following Saturday. Marek's emotions about the trip were confused. To visit Vienna had been enjoyable in all respects. He tried to make sense of his relationship to Maria, reflecting not only on her outburst about Jews but also on the cynical ways that she looked at small incidents in life. Their sex life was something which he could not have imagined before the trip. Although he enjoyed it and Maria's company, somehow the trip left an unpleasant feeling in him which he couldn't dispel. He knew that he didn't love Maria and he was sure she didn't love him. He put these thoughts to the back of his mind. They met only once more at a concert. The next time they were to meet she didn't show up. So after that he didn't contact her anymore and she didn't contact him.

Chapter Four

After the trip to Vienna, Marek made a short visit to his grandparents. He noted how they had aged since he last saw them a year ago. Jan was there, so they had several talks. Jan referred to their conversation of the previous year.

'I looked into what you told me about sales and costs. After analysing the sales I could not find any income for exports. I asked Grandad about this and he explained that money came in to the bank in different currencies, French and Swiss francs, pounds, dollars, and that these transfers from abroad went into a separate Foreign Currencies account at the bank. He kept all the relevant documentation in his office. He even said that without this the business would not be viable.

'Did Grandfather tell you how much the exports brought in?' asked Marek.

'No, he didn't. So we will just have to hope that it is enough to keep the business profitable. I probably won't know until I take over. Considering his health that should be arranged as soon as possible.'

It was in his fourth year at the University that Marek met Stefan. He had been talking with two friends one evening in a coffee house, all looking forward to the time when the Czech and Slovak lands would have their independence. Presently they were joined by an older man, perhaps thirty years old, who knew one of the group. He introduced himself as Stefan but did not give his surname. He said little but listened to the others, mainly Marek's diatribe about the emperor, 'that old fool Franz Josef.' When he got up to leave, Stefan gave Marek his address and asked him whether he could come to his rooms the following evening at seven o'clock.

Arriving on time, Stefan greeted Marek warmly. He was most interested in Marek's studies, his views of current affairs and the state of the empire. After breaking the ice in this way, Stefan spoke slowly and carefully.

'I share many of your views but I don't express them in public space as you did last evening. You were taking a big risk. Such views are considered by the regime as treacherous. State spies are everywhere. If a spy overheard you then you could be in serious trouble.'

He went on, 'Well, that was only one reason why I asked you to come here tonight. The other reason is for you to meet friends of mine. We all have the same motive – perhaps it could be called an obsession. We are planning for the independence of Bohemia, Moravia and Slovakia. I want you to consider joining us.'

Marek was amazed. He knew that others shared his vision but to meet a group seemed extraordinary to him.

A few minutes later, the door-bell rang and one after another eight men came in. One was the friend that Marek had been drinking with the previous evening. Marek was introduced to each one. They all seemed to know each other. Chatter continued for ten or fifteen minutes before Stefan asked for silence.

'Since we last met, I have been considering options. Many people who share our objectives think that some sort of independence can be achieved within the Habsburg empire – a sort of devolution of authority. Professor Masaryk is one of those people. I respect them but I do not agree with them.'

'I don't believe that the emperor, and more important, his advisers would ever grant us meaningful authority over our own lands. Furthermore the large minority of native German speakers in our provinces would fight any such proposals, and many of them are aristocrats who have connections in the highest places in Vienna and Budapest.'

'Well, if that is so, and I agree with your analysis, that leaves us only one alternative – Rebellion,' stated another, whose name Marek could not recall from the introductions.

Another man spoke, 'The state is too powerful. Our rebellion would be mercilessly crushed.'

'That is true today,' said Stefan. 'But circumstances can change. Look at Serbia. They are ready to rebel. God hold them back! They would be slaughtered. But let's take a long view, and I don't mean ten or twenty years but much sooner. The oppressed peoples outnumber Austrians and Hungarians. People are discontent with their lives. The empire is a fragile powder-keg. A spark could set it alight. When that happens we must be ready.'

'And how do we prepare?' asked another.

'I think we can do so in many ways. Let's each think about this and bring our ideas to our next meeting.'

Two weeks later the same group met again. Many thoughts were expressed by each man in turn. No specific decisions were taken but Stefan said that he wished to speak privately with each person. Then he collected all the notes and burned them.

It was not long before the two month summer vacation began. Marek needed to earn money to finance his final year. Stefan knew of a coalmine which always needed workers. He arranged for Marek to get a summer job there. So he went underground. The shift supervisor was an older man who took great care not to expose his men to unnecessary danger. He was glad to have the help of a literate worker and showed him how to use dynamite. The charge must be placed in just such a way, the correct length of fuse laid, timed and the dynamite detonated. Marek helped each time a charge had to be placed. At the end of the month he said good-bye to the supervisor, collected his pay and went home. He had learned what he wished to know.

Marek's studies were coming to a close in the summer of 1914 after four enjoyable years, studying hard and enjoying himself. The exams were over so he met up with three friends, members of Stefan's group, for a late lunch on June 28 to celebrate his twenty- second birthday. Just as they had almost finished the excellent, rather alcoholic lunch there was a commotion outside the restaurant. A man came in waving a newspaper and obviously distressed about something.

'Here it is in this paper – Archduke Franz Ferdinand and his wife have been assassinated in Sarajevo,' he blurted out.

News of the assassination of Archduke Franz Ferdinand and his wife Sophie shocked the world. They were on a visit to Sarajevo in Serbia, travelling through the town in a convoy in an open car.

Security was negligible. Seven assassins had spread out along the route, each ready to throw a bomb into the car. If one man failed to act the next in line would do so. The first man took fright and the car passed on. The second took a bomb from under his clothing, broke the detonator and threw it. It bounced off the back of the Archduke's car and exploded under the following vehicle which was crowded with officers and policemen. Several were injured but none died.

The assassin tried but failed to commit suicide. He crossed the embankment and jumped into the river but it was too shallow to drown him. Before he was arrested he swallowed part of a phial of cyanide but it was of poor quality and only made him ill. The Archduke actually helped organise the care of the injured before the convoy moved on to the town hall for speeches and celebrations.

On the return journey the Archduke's car took a wrong turning and had to be pushed back by policemen into the main road. At this point another terrorist, Gavrilo Principe was standing next to the car. He shot Franz Ferdinand and his wife at point-blank range. She died almost immediately and Franz Ferdinand soon after, despite efforts to save him.

The Archduke had been next in line to the throne after the Emperor Franz Josef, the elderly present Emperor who would surely die within a few years. He had had a son, Rudolf who died in mysterious circumstances. Officially his death occurred in a shooting accident, but no one believed this. His body was found in a lodge in Mayerling, along with his seventeen year-old lover, a Baroness. Papers later found in her safe deposit showed that she had planned the murder-suicide. That left Franz Josef's younger brother, Archduke Kurt Ludwig as heir to the throne, but he died before his elder brother, so that his son Archduke Franz Ferdinand was the next in line. The assassination meant that his young nephew, Archduke Karl was now the heir apparent.

The Emperor and all around him were furious and blamed the Serbian government which made only limited, inconclusive attempts to investigate the crime. They were further angered when the news was greeted with celebrations in the coffee houses of the Serbian capital and tactless articles appeared in the Serbian press.

Vienna was concerned that if they attacked Serbia then Russia might come to the aid of their orthodox 'little Slav brothers.' They concluded that they probably wouldn't do so.

It was crucial for Vienna to know whether Germany would support them. The Kaiser was initially cool but he and his advisers shared the Austrian view that Russia would probably not intervene. The Germans thought that if they did they could quickly defeat Russia. They knew that Russia was rapidly increasing its military capacity and that if war came in a few years' time then the outcome would be uncertain. If there was going to be a war then better now than later. The Austrians gave Serbia an ultimatum requiring very detailed onerous terms that they knew Serbia could not accept.

Chapter Five

Marek and his friends were so shocked by the news that they couldn't finish the meal that they had ordered. Each tried to take in the implications for the country and for themselves and their families. None of the group was married but they all had parents who were growing old and siblings. The big question everyone was asking - 'Will there be war with Serbia? And if so, what will Russia do?.' They had no answers but many opinions. The four friends agreed on one thing – they had to find Stefan.

He was not at home. So they sat in a coffee house near to his rooms where they could see the entrance to his building. The place was quite full of people but it was strangely quiet. At each table people talked in low tones and many were silent.

After an hour Stefan returned. One of them, Adam, spotted him and ran out to welcome him and asked him to join them. Stefan declined but asked them to come up to his rooms, but in groups of two, three minutes apart. The men shook their heads. Stefan was developing paranoia about being followed and arrested.

Seated comfortably with glasses of beer in their hands, the group slowly started to talk of the implications of the terrible news. The conversation was similar to that taking place all over Europe. All agreed that there would be some sort of military offensive. Whether there would be a formal declaration of war was unclear. Would events lead to intervention by Russia? They thought it would do so. Whatever happened there would be a crackdown on liberties which would cause more unrest and uprisings throughout the fragile Habsburg empire.

Stefan summed up the situation by saying that this might be the chance that they were waiting for to rise up against their oppressors. 'We must wait and see.'

'It is common knowledge that Archduke Franz Ferdinand disagreed with Emperor Franz Josef about policy for the minority peoples. The Emperor had alternately ignored and then oppressed the Czechs, Slovaks, Serbs and others. Franz Ferdinand had studied the American constitution and proposed to the Emperor a federation of semi-independent states within the Habsburg empire. When he tried to talk with his uncle, the old man wouldn't listen and it is said that he became angry.'

'So it is a tragedy that it was the heir to the throne, Archduke Franz Ferdinand who was assassinated,' said Adam.

'Yes, but it was probably too late, the minority peoples were close to revolt and it would have been only a matter of time before there would be uprisings all across the empire,' Stefan concluded. 'It may be several years before the old man dies and every year it would become more likely that there would be uprisings. Now, after the assassination, and the likely coming war there is no chance of continuing with the oppression and a federated empire is impossible.'

The conversation turned to their own personal concerns. If there was war with Russia they would all be liable to be conscripted into the army, except Radek who was extremely short-sighted. What were their options?

'I would rather fight for Russia against the Habsburg monarchy than against Russia,' said Samuel. If Russia wins we will have our independence as a free Czech nation.'

'Perhaps,' added David, 'but what will be the position of Germany? The Kaiser and his thugs would never let Franz Josef down. He would certainly intervene. And where do Britain and France stand?'

'Well, a lot will happen but tonight we don't know what it will be. Let's just follow events in the newspapers and keep out of trouble. We can meet again soon. In the next days I will be away from Prague but I'll send you all a message as to when we could meet,' said Stefan. They left, one by one.

Nothing much happened in the next days except the spread of rumours. So Marek went home to Zlin where the family were full of fears for the future. There was plenty to be fearful about. If war came, all young men would be recruited, including Marek. He didn't tell them that whatever happened he was not going to serve in the Austria-Hungarian army. The fact is he didn't know himself what viable option was available.

So Veronika proposed to him that they should make a short visit to her parents. They were greeted warmly. Both were surprised that her father, now in his sixties, didn't think that the situation was dangerous.

'Oh, it will all blow over,' he assured them.

Marek didn't like to disabuse his grandfather so he said nothing. His wife had no opinion to offer. The visitors took the train home after only two days.

As soon as the ultimatum became public knowledge – even though it had not been officially announced – Marek returned to Prague. He found Stefan who wished to call a meeting of the group. When they met the following day all were grim faced. Stefan quickly came to the point.

'In my view it is certain that Serbia will not agree to the Vienna proposals, which amount to an ultimatum. So Austria-Hungary will invade Serbia, with or without a formal declaration of war. That will bring in Russia and probably Germany on the side of Austria-Hungary. I have taken a personal decision. If there is war, I will fight on the Russian side. If Russia wins, we will declare independence in Bohemia, Moravia and Slovakia.'

Several others said that they would do the same. A few were silent.

Marek was fully aware of the decision that he would soon have to take. He decided to make another trip home which he knew might be the last visit for a long time. Perhaps that would clear his head but he had no intention of telling them that he might go to fight for Russia. He would simply disappear.

On arrival he found that his parents had no illusions about the gravity of the situation. Pavel was well and his mind was clear. He told Marek of an incident which occurred the previous day.

A few days after Vienna had given Belgrade the ultimatum which Austria knew the Serbs would never accept, two men walked into Tomas Bata's office where he was discussing a shoe design problem with Pavel. The taller of the two men wore a military uniform. He spoke in German.

'I assume that you are Tomas Bata,' a question phrased as a statement.

'I am,' confirmed Bata.

'I am Colonel Merkel and this is Herr Meyer. We have come to inform you that your factory has been requisitioned by the state. You will remain the owner and manager but production will be decided by Herr Meyer, acting on behalf of the state which will be your only customer. At this stage I can only tell you that production of shoes will cease and your factory will only manufacture boots for the army. You will be paid a fair price. Is this clear?'

It was only too clear to Tomas Bata and he was speechless. He only managed to nod his head, signifying that he had understood.

'You will receive further instructions in a few days. You will also receive the official notification of what I have just told you. In the next ten days you will prepare a list of your employees giving their gender and date of birth. Include those working for you from their homes who are not formally employees.'

With that the visitors walked out without another word. Pavel followed them out to see them getting into the back seat of a car and being driven away.

This story finally convinced Marek that war was inevitable. He returned to Prague.

Serbia sent a polite but evasive answer to the ultimatum which Vienna took as a refusal, so on July 28, 1914 Austria-Hungary declared war. There followed in rapid succession, within one week, declarations of war across Europe. Germany and Austria-Hungary declared war on Russia, Belgium and France, then the British Empire on Germany and Austria-Hungary. Later in August Japan joined in, declaring war on Germany and Austria-Hungary. So the protagonists were lined up – the Central Powers comprising Germany and Austria-Hungary and later the Ottoman Empire, opposed by Russia, France, the British Empire, Belgium and later Italy - known as the Entente. The United States of America remained neutral.

The people of Europe went happily to war, expecting that it would 'all be over by Christmas.' The popular press of many countries had encouraged an atmosphere of aggressive nationalism which leaders supported. Few foresaw the dangers of industrialised warfare. The nations of Europe were sleepwalking into the greatest carnage the world had ever seen.

The assassination of the heir to the thrones of Austria and Hungary was only a spark which set-off the declarations of war. There were many causes. Russia and Austria-Hungary were suspicious of each other's intentions in south-eastern Europe, where the Slav population was angry with the oppression by the Austrians and Hungarians. Germany was ruled by the arrogant Kaiser Wilhelm III who had a belligerent attitude to diplomacy. Britain and Germany were locked in an arms race. The British, alarmed at Germany's growing strength and its collaboration with Austria - Hungary, had signed treaties with Russia and France, which was still smarting from the loss to Germany of its two border provinces of Alsace and Lorraine.

The Ottoman Empire had been disintegrating for many years. Britain ruled Egypt and Italy captured Libya. The European powers squabbled about the Ottoman lands. In 1912 a group of countries, Bulgaria, Greece, Montenegro and Serbia captured the Ottoman possessions in the Balkans, further showing the weakness of the Ottoman empire.

On the evening when the war was declared the whole group met again. Stefan made his situation clear.

'There is no direct way to get to Russia from Prague. When I was away I secretly went to the Polish border. Contacts there informed me of a considerable number of Czechs and Slovaks in Russia who intend to join the Russian army. In fact, they intend to create a Czech and Slovak brigade within the Russian army.

I intended to find a possible way across the border to the eastern part of Poland where I could then make contact with the Russian army. I now know how and where this could be done. It would be dangerous but quite possible. So I have made all the necessary arrangements and I am going to leave to-morrow morning.'

He paused to allow the group to take in the gravity of what he had said.

'Does anyone wish to join me?'

They knew the alternative – serving in the Austrian army. There was silence. Slowly hands were raised in acceptance by all except Radek, who was sure that if he remained his very poor eyesight would keep him out of the army.

Chapter Six

Marek didn't sleep well that night. On the one hand he wanted to tell his parents what he was doing and to explain why. However, he couldn't write to them because if the letter were to fall into the hands of an official, or even a supporter of the monarchy, his parents could be in serious trouble. Unaccustomed to doing so, he said a quiet prayer when dressing. Then he quickly ate breakfast, made a few sandwiches, dropped the room keys in the letter box of the landlady and went to join his comrades.

Stefan split the group of ten into five teams of two. The teams were to keep well apart as they walked but if they came into close contact as they approached the meeting place, they were to ignore each other. They must travel light, carrying a few possessions, a packed lunch and a bottle of water. They must appear to be on a day trip until they would meet up at an agreed spot in a small town outside Prague. So they left the city early in the beautiful, clear morning and all found their way to the meeting place. Stefan recognised the man he had contracted, at considerable expense, to take them in a truck to their destination. All ten lay down in the back of the open truck for the five-hour journey to an old, empty farmhouse where they could sleep overnight. It was close to the Polish border, a long way from Prague, but where they could reach the Russian occupied part of Poland. Crossing the nearest border north of Prague would have brought them into German controlled Poland.

In the evening an old peasant woman appeared with provisions and went into the kitchen to prepare a delicious goulash. They all slept fitfully on the wooden floor, tired from the long journey. It would have been possible to cross the mountain that night but Stefan wished everyone to rest before what would certainly be a strenuous climb and they had no idea what dangers they would face on the other side of the mountain.

The next morning the woman appeared again and cooked for them. Marek watched as Stefan counted out lots of coins into her hand and the old lady actually smiled. When they had all washed and eaten breakfast, Stefan called a meeting.

'So far, so good,' he summed up the previous day's journey. 'Tonight we must cross into the Russian-controlled part of Poland. We will meet up with a farmer who knows the route over the mountain and he will be our guide. I met him last week. It will be dangerous for him as well as for us, so he will turn back before we meet anyone. He estimates that the climb and descent will take about five hours. It will be dark most of the way.

When we see the lights of a border post or other occupied buildings we will wait until dawn before making contact, just in-case a guard panics on seeing us and opens fire. I am not sure how Poles would receive us. They dislike their occupiers, the Russians, so if they know that we intend to join the Russian army they may be hostile. The situation is likely to be changing daily so I don't know whether the border posts will be staffed by Poles or Russians. We must avoid the border posts and try to find a Russian army patrol or base. Any questions?'

'Should we walk in pairs or all together?' asked Adam.

'We must keep close together to be sure that we don't get separated in the dark,' replied Stefan. 'All right then. Today we must stay in the house or in the enclosed space at the back. It's hot, so drink plenty of water and get what rest you can,' he concluded.

They were ready at ten o'clock when the farmer arrived. He gave only brief instructions.

'Follow me in single file. And don't talk!' was all he said.

The climb was long and the path narrow and rugged. At first they .stumbled often but by midnight the moon was shining and they made good progress, taking a short break every hour. Marek could see the outline of the mountain peaks and he imagined what a wonderful hike it would be in daytime and in other circumstances.

Eventually they could see the lights of a village in the distance so they stopped. The farmer said good-bye and turned back so that he could reach his farm before daybreak.They had brought bread, ham and cheese. They had no idea what might happen that day but this might be their only meal.

After daybreak Stefan went ahead into the village together with Marek. Neither spoke Russian but they hoped to find someone in authority who could speak at least some basic English or German. They soon saw a police station with two policemen on guard. Stefan and Marek walked slowly and then crawled, getting near to them to hear what they were saying. The guards were laughing and joking in a language they did not understand. Polish is similar to Czech and they were not speaking Polish nor German so it was probably Russian. They now approached them with their hands above their heads to show that they were unarmed.

The policemen raised but then lowered their rifles and called out to another one to come out. The conversation could have been between deaf people. Apparently they were not policemen but Russian soldiers. By signs the soldiers indicated that Stefan and Marek would be taken to the nearest town and handed over to their commander. Stefan shouted loudly to the others to join them, hands above their heads. The soldiers were clearly taken by surprise at the appearance of eight more men who they assumed at first were Polish. One soldier searched them for weapons while the other two covered him with their rifles.

They marched for nearly an hour, one soldier leading and the other following at the rear where he could keep an eye on the captives.

If the commander was surprised by the arrival of the group he didn't show it. The guards explained the sudden appearance of the ten men. The commander addressed them in Russian but they didn't understand and couldn't reply.

'*Sprechen Sie Deutsch*? Do you speak English?' asked Marek.

Now the commander was surprised. After a moment or two he replied in broken English.

'Who you are, where you from, and where you go?'

Marek explained slowly in English, concluding: 'We have come to join the Russian army and to fight against her enemies.'

'Wait here.' He went inside and came out after half an hour.

'You are arrested. I take you to army base.'

Twenty minutes later several more armed men in uniform arrived in two trucks. The prisoners were told to get on the trucks, five on each, and several guards got on. The journey to the city took over an hour. When they arrived at the army base it was clear that they were expected. They were shown into a bare room with a few benches. A few minutes later an officer arrived, clearly of high rank, probably, thought Marek, a colonel judging by his uniform. He spoke excellent German and English.

'What is your story?' he demanded.

Stefan gave a long explanation in German, in which he emphasised that they wished to join the Russian army. The colonel, if he was one, listened carefully and asked only twice for confirmation of what was said. Finally, he replied in fluent German.

'I welcome you to Russia. I am aware that many other Czechs and Slovaks wish to do as you wish to do and that there are plans to form them all into a separate brigade within the Russian army. I will find out more about this but it may take a few days because the situation is changing daily. In the meantime you may stay here as our guests. You will not be prisoners but you must remain on the base.'

'Sergeant, find space in a barrack room and get these men some food,' he commanded, and left the room.

The days passed without incident. The barrack rooms and meals were very much what they expected and the soldiers were friendly. Marek took every opportunity to learn Russian by talking to the soldiers, which he knew would be essential when they joined the Russian army. To pass the time they played chess. When the soldiers were off duty several challenged Stefan and Marek to a game. They were strong players and usually won. On Sunday they were taken to Church. The service seemed monotonous and they didn't understand a word. They stood up and knelt down following the rest of the congregation. Marek found a certain quiet beauty in the unaccompanied singing.

Ten days passed before the group was called into the same room where the officer had spoken to them on arrival. He soon appeared and spoke to them in German.

'You may know that Russia is at war with Germany and Austria-Hungary.' They had heard this from Russian soldiers.

'The Russian high command has authorised the formation of a brigade of Czech and Slovak volunteers to be formed. You may join this brigade. Tomorrow you will be taken under guard to the headquarters of the Russian

Third Army where the battalion is being formed. I wish you well,' and he left without inviting questions.

True to his word, two trucks arrived at dawn. The ten men were told to get aboard and the journey started. They had no idea where in Russia they were heading. After about two hours they reached the border between Russian occupied Poland and Russia itself – actually Ukraine, which was effectively part of the Russian empire.

Again they were in for a surprise. After about thirty minutes they arrived at a large town and were driven to a railway station. Here they were handed over to railway police, drivers and guards wishing them well as they turned round for the drive back to their barracks. Marek and his fellow Czechs were escorted to a train and they settled down in a carriage which must have been third class. Seats were hard and the train crowded with peasants travelling east. After about two hours they changed trains. The two guards made no attempt to guard them, assuming correctly that they didn't wish to escape and there was nowhere to escape to anyway. Finally, they arrived at what was obviously a major army base.

Chapter Seven

Following the outbreak of war Professor Masaryk continued to live in Prague and to carry on activities against the regime's war effort. He setup a spy network with informers in key ministries in Vienna. Friends persuaded him that he was in danger of arrest and imprisonment, so he and his adult daughter Olga took the train to the Italian border and using forged passports slipped into Italy. From there he went on to France, Britain, Canada, the USA and then later to Switzerland.

It was now clear to him that the prospect of a federal system in the Habsburg empire was an illusion. He must convince the Entente governments to support independence for the minority peoples of the empire. With a few enthusiastic colleagues he intended to lobby the politicians and to inform and educate the public as to how the authorities in Vienna oppressed the minority who had a democratic right to govern themselves.

They were followed by spies everywhere and eventually an arrest warrant was issued for Masaryk *in absentia*. He already had many high level contacts. including friendships with editors of major newspapers. He was enthusiastic for the deployment of a Czechoslovak Legion in France and then in Russia. He correctly concluded that this would reinforce demands for independence when the war ended, that is if Austria-Hungary were defeated. With all this in mind Masaryk and his colleagues established the Czecho-Slovak National Council which came gradually to be recognised by the Entente as a government-in-exile.

In 1914 there were many first and second generation Czechs and Slovaks living in France, the United States and Canada and some in Britain and Italy. They were keen to fight and the French army was keen to have them.

In some respects their group was similar to the French Foreign Legion, so they got the name 'Czechoslovak Legion' in France and later in Italy and Russia. They served with distinction on the western front throughout the war.

From the beginning of the nineteenth century, the industry of Russia had been growing in size and sophistication. Many well educated foreigners, including Czechs and Slovaks, had been attracted by job opportunities in western Russia and they were now cut off from their homeland. Some had brought their families with them and others had married local women. Almost all of them were anti-Habsburg monarchy and now saw the longed for opportunity for the lands of Bohemia, Moravia, Slovakia and others to gain independence.

The Czechs and Slovaks quickly petitioned the Tsarist government to support their wishes for the independence of their lands. In return they volunteered to fight for Russia against the Central Powers. They recommended the establishment of a brigade of volunteers within the Russian army. On August 15, 1914, the authorities approved the formation of such a group known as the *Družina* in Russian, or Czech and Slovak 'companions.'

Stefan and his group were well received at the large army base that they soon discovered was the headquarters of the Russian Third Army. They were taken to barracks which were full of many Czechs and a few Slovaks, volunteers from all over western Russia. After brief interviews they were assigned to platoons for six weeks of intense military training given by three experienced Czech soldiers. Only a very few recruits had army experience.

The exercises were physically demanding, especially over obstacle courses, and some of the older trainees were exhausted every evening. But all the recruits became very fit. There was training in the use of various weapons and lectures on the practical aspects of infantry work, such as how to set an ambush and how to escape from one. They practised digging trenches and were taught how to survive in them. They were taught how to use a compass to march at night to a designated objective, how to capture an enemy soldier who could be interrogated for crucial information.

When the training was complete a rank was assigned to each soldier, apparently based on the reports of the instructors and the details each soldier had given about himself. Adam was given the rank of sergeant. Stefan and Marek became lieutenants. They went on to three weeks of training for officers which included military strategy, instruction in the deployment of heavy weapons, the use and dangers of dynamite and the problems of keeping frontline troops supplied with ammunition and food during extended combat.

The *Družina* grew only slowly. Many Czech and Slovak soldiers were captured or had deserted the Austrian army. For some inexplicable reason these prisoners of war were kept in prison camps and not allowed to join the army as they were keen to do. Apparently the Tsar and his advisers could not bear the thought of men who once wore enemy uniforms serving in the Russian army and wearing Russian army uniforms. Or perhaps they doubted that they would be loyal and not give away secret information to the enemy if they allowed themselves to be captured.

Despite protestations from *Družina* commanders, many senior Russian officers and representatives at Entente headquarters in France, including Masaryk, the restriction continued in force. Unfortunately potential volunteers in the camps were abused by Austrian and Hungarian officers, sometimes even murdered.

Marek was now involved in various tasks, such as reconnaissance, capture and interrogation of prisoners. He could speak to prisoners in Czech or German and so gained useful information which he passed up the line to senior officers who valued his reports. He was even able to prevent a few prisoners from being taken to a prison camp and to recruit them to the Legion. Local Russian commanders knew what was happening and turned a blind eye to it.

Russian Third Army units made only limited gains whereas *Družina* troops made inroads into Austrian held territory. Marek's unit overran a regional Austrian headquarters. It couldn't be held so the Legion captured valuable stores, weapons and ammunition and took prisoners. With the help of two soldiers, Marek laid dynamite to the huge store of ammunitions which they couldn't transport. There were four separate sections to the arsenal. Marek and his soldiers set a separate charge to each store, timed to go off simultaneously. They waited until all their colleagues had left before lighting the fuses and running away themselves. The explosion could be seen and heard from a long way away.

The official report of this incident led to Marek's promotion to captain. It was his character to take risks and with growing self-confidence he began taking unnecessary ones.

The exploits of the *Družina* came to the attention of General Dieterikhs, a much decorated Russian officer serving in the Third Army. He took personal command of the Czechs and Slovaks and supported them in all their contacts with the Russian authorities and he was tireless in his advocacy of allowing prisoners to join the army.

The war was not going well for the Entente on either the western or eastern fronts. In the first weeks the German army units came close to entering Paris. They were stopped and both sides dug-in. From then on, for four years the opposing armies dug trenches, eventually from the Swiss border to the English channel. Millions died as heavy machine guns and poison gas were used and tanks were seen for the first time in major battles. Each side gained and then lost small areas of land, to no advantage but at huge cost in lives and materials. Villages and towns were demolished.

In the east the situation of the Russian army became dire as they fought against the combined forces of Germany and Austria-Hungary. In the heavy losses incurred in the first battles a large majority of the junior officers, perhaps seventy per cent, were killed or wounded. These men were mainly competent, highly trained young aristocrats who were replaced by promoted uneducated soldiers who lacked the necessary training and abused those they commanded. The ordinary soldiers hated them as much as the enemy. There were even rumours of soldiers deliberately shooting their own officers in the back during the heat of battle. Many soldiers went into battle sharing only one rifle between three and with little ammunition, without warm clothing and adequate food. Desertions began.

Famine began to spread among the masses in the cities and fuel was in short supply. The peasants now in the army or in the factories were away from the farms. There was widespread corruption and wealthier peasants and traders were accused of hoarding the limited produce in the hope of getting a better price on the black market. The rich continued to squander their wealth, attending concerts, plays and extravagant balls in St Petersburg and Moscow.

The Tsar was blamed for not leading his people and was widely disliked. His wife the Tsarina was of German origin and stories circulated that she was a secret German supporter and even a spy. She was influenced by a strange character, Grigory Rasputin, a mystic from Siberia who claimed to have healing powers which could help the young crown prince Alexis, who suffered from severe attacks of haemophilia.

Several people, including a grand duke, princes and generals tried to persuade the Tsar to send the Tsarina away – anywhere out of the limelight. It could be to his cousin, King George V and his family in London. Either he refused or she refused to go and leave her sick child.

Tsar Nicholas replaced the general commanding the army, Grand Duke Nikolai Nikolaevich and took over the command himself. He had no qualifications or experience which would have fitted him for this role. This might not have mattered had he listened to his advisers but he ignored all advice, constantly changing his mind, giving orders and then cancelling them. Soldiers and civilians, including many aristocrats, now blamed the Tsar personally for military reverses and the deplorable conditions in the army. In his absence at the front his wife the Tsarina and Rasputin virtually ran the country. In December 1916 monarchists murdered Rasputin. The royal family went into mourning.

The *Družina* continued to hold their ground in Ukraine as the German and Austrian armies advanced and Russian units retreated or simply fled in disorder. Marek was in command of a company which was taking heavy losses. On March 15, 1916 a bullet went into his left arm near the shoulder and it began to bleed profusely. Two soldiers carried him back to a Red Cross team who took him to a Russian field hospital. By then he had lost consciousness.

Chapter Eight

The bed in the field hospital was urgently needed as more wounded arrived so a week after his operation Marek walked out, with his arm bandaged and in a sling. Before leaving he had an appointment with the surgeon who had operated on him.

'The bullet entered just below the shoulder and caused a lot of damage. I'm afraid you will not recover use of that arm. The Red Cross team saved your life but you lost a lot of blood and it will be several weeks before you get your strength back. So in the meantime try not to exert yourself unduly. And here is a souvenir of your stay here. Good luck.'

He handed Marek a small roll of newspaper. Inside was a bullet.

'Thank you for everything,' replied Marek. After thanking and saying good bye to the nurses he returned to his unit. Still weak and with the use of only one arm there was no possibility that he could return to active service. His fighting days were over and he was given a series of minor office jobs which he performed competently but with little enthusiasm. He slowly regained strength.

The Tsar partially relented from his outright ban on releasing prisoners of war from camps to allow them to work in ammunition factories. This was not a big improvement as conditions in the factories were little better than slavery. Despite continuous pleas from many groups the prohibition from them joining the army remained. Influential factory owners lobbied to keep their free workers.

The military situation deteriorated and the war became unpopular. The British and French governments were desperate to keep the Russians in the war and they continued to send large quantities of supplies. This was hazardous. The northern ports of Murmansk and Archangel were frequently ice-bound and the approaching ships were in danger from German submarines and mines. Shipments to the ice-free port of Vladivostok on the Pacific ocean were far from the battle front where they were needed. Some seventy German and Austrian divisions were tied down in Russia and if they were transferred to the western front the balance of power there would change radically. But Russia was on the point of revolution.

Food shortages and deteriorating conditions caused an uprising by soldiers and sailors in February 1917 in St Petersburg. This unrest spread to other places, including both the army, navy and the factory workers. Tsar Nicholas panicked and fearing for his life and his family, he abdicated the throne in favour of his brother, Grand Duke Mikhail Alexandrovich. But he prevaricated, first accepting with conditions, then refusing the throne. The Duma, or Parliament, took over and eventually a prominent member, Alexander Kerensky became the leader of a Provisional Government. Kerensky took the Tsar and his family into custody for their protection against mobs.

Chaos in the towns and cities continued and spread to the countryside. The Duma promised a commission to plan land reform but the peasants were not prepared to wait. Their life had not changed much since the abolition of serfdom. They hated the owners of the big estates. First they took the land. Then, encouraged by visiting rioters from the cities they ransacked and burnt the huge properties and chased the owners and their families away. Many aristocrats fled south to Odessa while others supported the Provisional Government in its efforts to restore order. But it was too late.

Kerensky ordered a major offensive which initially took the Austrian-Hungarian commanders by surprise. A major breakthrough occurred at the small town of Zborov where several thousand prisoners were taken and many weapons and large quantities of ammunition were captured by the Czechoslovak *Družina*. Unfortunately German reinforcements counterattacked and the Russian army retreated in disorder.

Czech and Slovak soldiers fought valiantly in the offensive but their efforts were not sufficient to make the attack a success. Kerensky recognised their bravery and strategic abilities and he dropped all remaining restrictions on the recruitment of prisoners. Consequently the *Družina* was quickly transformed into a major fighting force and became known as the Czechoslovak Legion. The new recruits swore allegiance to Czechoslovakia, a country that didn't yet exist!

The Austrian-Hungarian army had been severely damaged by the mauling they had taken and by desertions and the German high command became convinced of what they had suspected – that their 'partners' could not be relied on. Seven divisions had to be kept at home by Vienna to deal with uprisings by minorities.

Despite this setback and the clear wishes of the majority of the Russian people Kerensky still considered that the obviously unwinnable war should continue, encouraged by the Entente governments and the declaration of war against the Central Powers by the United States on April 6, 1917. The soldiers and sailors had had enough; they simply put down the few weapons that they held and fled. The Russian armed forces had disintegrated.

Masaryk was in Russia on a lengthy visit. He organised a group of officers to visit POW camps to interview recruits to the Legion. Marek, his strength and energy now recovered was assigned to this group, so with a small staff he set up a makeshift office in one of the larger camps.

Many Czech and Slovak prisoners did not know what was happening in the world outside their camp. When they understood many were enthusiastic to join. Marek had to be careful not to take in pro-Habsburg potential spies. Pro-Habsburg prisoners, many of them officers, were openly hostile to him and his staff but although there was no violence these people frequently caused disruption to the work. Marek carried a loaded revolver for his own protection – just in case.

Vladimir Ilyich Ulyanov, who later preferred the name Lenin was the son of a minor aristocrat. Lenin was eight when his elder brother was arrested and executed for leading a socialist uprising. This had a profound effect on the boy. He studied the writings of Marx and Engels and became a fervent socialist. He regarded capitalism and capitalists as wicked and he vowed to work for a world taken over by workers and peasants, to be managed for their benefit after the elimination of capitalists and the structures of capital and of all kings and emperors. This included the church. All monasteries would be confiscated and closed.

Lenin was a brilliant law student but his career in law was interrupted by periods of imprisonment. He went abroad, moving from one country to another where he continued to study and plot revolution.

His biographer, Louis Fischer described him:

'Lenin's collected writings reveal in detail a man with iron will, self-enslaving self-discipline, scorn for opponents and obstacles, the cold determination of a zealot, the drive of a fanatic, and the ability to convince or browbeat weaker persons by his singleness of purpose,

imposing intensity, impersonal approach, personal sacrifice, political astuteness, and complete
conviction of the possession of the absolute truth. His life became the history of the Bolshevik movement.'

Lenin's future comrade at the head of the Bolshevik movement, Lev Davidovich Bronstein was born into a moderately wealthy Jewish family in 1879. The family were not orthodox Jews and did not speak Yiddish at home. Young Bronstein had a rebellious nature and his activities in banned socialist groups earned him four years hard labour in 1900. He escaped, travelling to London assuming the name of one of his guards, Leon Trotsky, the name he used for the rest of his life.

In London he met Lenin. They had many talks about the way forward for socialism. The socialist movement was splitting between the Bolsheviks supported by Lenin and the Mensheviks, a group which adhered to Karl Marx's view that socialism should lead in steps to communism. Lenin, on the other hand, wished to establish communism across the world immediately by wiping out all opposition.

Trotsky agreed with him. He spent many years writing, speaking, being imprisoned, escaping again and travelling to many countries, organising and reporting on uprisings. He worked with Lenin in Switzerland, moved on to France from where he was deported to Spain, USA and then Canada. When he received news of the Tsar's abdication Trotsky returned to Russia.

On hearing of the February uprising at his home in neutral Switzerland Lenin became determined to get to Russia. This would involve crossing Germany which was still at war with Russia. He made contact with the German authorities and they arranged for Lenin, his wife and thirty friends to be smuggled in a sealed train via Sweden and Finland into St Petersburg. The Germans hoped that he would cause trouble for Russia and they were not disappointed.

Lenin and his colleagues, Trotsky and their young *protégé* thug Josef Stalin, calling themselves Bolsheviks, raised supporters and in November they invaded the Winter Palace in St Petersburg where members of the Provisional Government were meeting. They seized power in a bloodless counter revolution, overthrowing the Provisional Government headed by Kerensky. The red flag flew over the Winter Palace. The rioters 'liberated' the Tsar's wine cellars and their drunken orgy lasted three days.

Almost the first act of the Bolsheviks was the very popular decision to take Russia out of the war. After the ceasefire negotiations a treaty was eventually signed at Brest-Litovsk, in which Germany imposed punitive conditions. Russia lost huge areas of land, industry and people.

The end of the war in the east had enormous repercussions. Many entire divisions of German and Austrian troops were re-deployed to France, taking their weapons and equipment with them. Many troops still loyal to the Tsar fought against those who supported Lenin's still very weak soviet units. Lenin's group of socialist Bolsheviks were more extreme than Kerensky's people. These three groups began to fight each other. The Czechs and Slovaks tried to remain neutral under pressure to take sides, maintaining that they 'hadn't come to Russia to kill Russians.'

The guards at the prison camps simply went away, leaving the prisoners without food but free to leave. They were faced with several options, none very attractive. The Germans were organising trains to take them to Germany and then to the front in France. Or they could walk home – without footwear or adequate clothing and not knowing how to feed themselves on the journey. Or they could join the expanding Red Army, with promises of a warm uniform and food. This group became known as the ' Internationalists.' The final option was to join the Legion.

With Russia out of the war the Legion's leaders and the men wished only to get to a port, get aboard a ship and either go to fight in France or go home. Getting to a port, either the northern ones or Vladivostok would be difficult and in some places they would have to fight their way through.

It was already cold in October 1917 in Ukraine. The summer had been warm but now there were already light snow showers. Marek pulled the scarf tighter around his throat as he walked over to the General's boxcar. He was early for his appointment at four o'clock, anxious not to be a minute late. Marek's knock on the door was answered by a sergeant who let him in.

'I have an appointment with the General at four o'clock,' he informed the sergeant.

'Yes, Captain Novak. The General is not here at the moment but he will be back very soon. Can I offer you a hot tea while you wait?'

'Thank you, that would be very pleasant.'

At a couple of minutes to four o'clock, the General arrived, accompanied by a young lieutenant.

'Ah, Novak, come into my office. Bring your cup of tea with you.'

Marek had only met the General briefly about a year ago when he was reviewing troops but his manner suggested that he remembered him. He had no idea why he had been called in. But the General's friendly greeting reassured Marek that the objective was not to discipline him.

The General had a file open in front of him to which he referred.

'Have you fully recovered from your injury?' he enquired.

'Yes, thank God. The arm is now rather useless but the pain has gone, and I have recovered strength after losing a lot of blood.'

'Good, I see that it is your left arm. Are you right handed?' the General asked.

'Yes, so I can write and perform my clerical duties without difficulty,' Marek assured him.

'Excellent. I have received good reports from your Colonel about you. I want you to join my staff. You will be responsible to Colonel Kucera. The administrative burden of the incorporation of the prisoners into the Legion is going to be overwhelming. These men are weak. They need solid food and medical attention before we can expect them to fight. I want you to come immediately. I will inform your Colonel.'

'I will be honoured to serve under you ....' Marek was too embarrassed to use the generally adopted style of 'Brother' which had replaced 'Sir' throughout the Legion. So he said neither and the sentence was left unfinished. After all, the General was about twice his age and five ranks senior.

'Oh, yes. For the work you will be doing you need to have a higher rank. I am promoting you to Major, with immediate effect. Get a new uniform. The Lieutenant here will see to the paper work.'

It was clear that the interview was over. Marek, now Major Novak, saluted and left the boxcar.

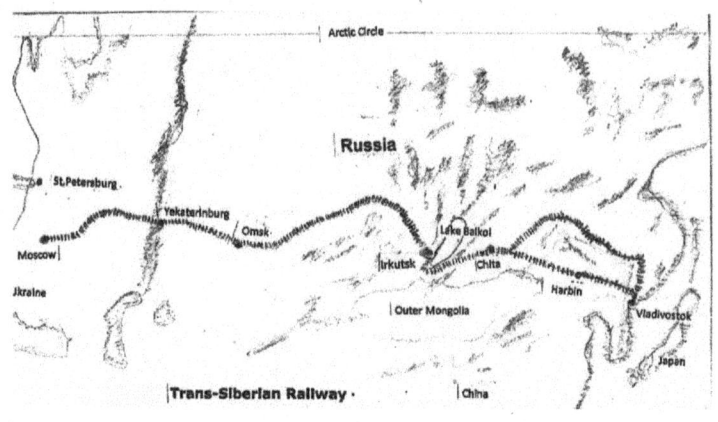

Chapter Nine

Russian Tsars had expanded their territory to the east for hundreds of years. The ill-defined area, known as Siberia had been occupied by tribes such as the Buryats and Mongols for centuries before Russia tried to colonise it. Siberia is a vast inhospitable land. The northern regions, stretching to the arctic are frozen all the year round. The southern part is habitable, at least by the hardy. Temperatures vary from -20°C to -70°C in the long winter, and up to +20°C in the short summer. Strong winds during even a light snowfall could cause drifts which were more than the height of a man.

In the late nineteenth and early twentieth centuries many Russians chose to seek their fortune in Siberia, as well as convicts who did not choose their exile. They did not find a totally inhospitable land. There were herds of reindeer and other animals such as wild boar, wolf and bear and the rivers teemed with fish. Journeys had always been difficult in Siberia. Winter was usually the best time to travel – in summer the swollen rivers created a vast, impenetrable sea of mud.

By the mid-nineteenth century, Russia had established control over the southern route but communications were still a major problem. An official taking up his post in a distant settlement could travel on horseback for two years to reach his destination. Messages to dead state employees were never delivered and couriers were often intercepted by bandits.

Tsar Alexander III decided to open up Siberia and in 1891 he announced the building of a railway to cross Russia. He was inspired by the recently constructed Union Pacific line from Chicago to San Francisco. This railway was already contributing to the rapid development of the states which it crossed and the hope was that the same thing would happen in Siberia. The Tsar foresaw that the railway would solve some of Russia's social and economic problems and establish Russia as a great power.

The proclamation was widely welcomed but was short on detail. No route was precisely described, costs were not published, engineering technicalities were left for later determination. The Tsar was determined that this would be a Russian project, Russian designed and constructed by Russians. Only finance would come from abroad, since the sums required exceeded anything in the Russian treasury. A very large loan issued in Paris was still not sufficient for the project. It was subscribed by rich people and institutions in many countries with only minimum fraud.

Following the American example of starting construction at both ends and meeting somewhere near the middle, the Russians began work in Moscow and Vladivostok. There was already a rudimentary though quite extensive rail network in western Russia, with antiquated equipment and rolling stock. There was a line linking St Petersburg with Moscow.

The ill thought-through project was enormous, some 10,000 kms/6,200 miles long. It was far longer even than the American line and crossed huge rivers, mountain ranges and through vast forests and had to circumvent a big expanse of water, Lake Baikal. Many experts dismissed the whole project as impossible. The climate severely restricted the time when work could be done. To meet the ten- year deadline imposed by the Tsar, the line was split into six more or less equal sections which were to be worked on at the same time.

Funds were restricted so costs were cut by using inferior materials and employing unskilled labour, convicts and later Chinese. Iron, not steel, was used for tracks and many smaller bridges were built of wood rather than stone and steel. Engineers used their discretion in varying the route for the track where carrying out the plan proved to be impossible. Using local materials posed problems. Larchwood proved unsuitable for sleepers and in most sections there were no stones for ballast.

The first section of the line over the Ural mountains from Moscow to Yekaterinburg existed. From there, across the flat steppe, rails were simply laid on the ground, so that rapid progress was made and Omsk was reached. From there on progress was much slower, across a vast swamp.

Both routes ended on either side of the huge Lake Baikal which was surrounded by high mountains. Equipment, locomotives and even ice breakers arrived in pieces travelling by sea across the Indian ocean to Vladivostok. Then by train or by horse and cart where the train had not yet been constructed, the equipment arrived where it was needed and was assembled from the parts. This was inefficient. If a part was missing or damaged it could take six months to get a replacement.

The biggest challenge of all was how to get passed the enormous Lake Baikal. Equipment and people could be moved by boat but the lake froze over during the long winters. It took six years to dig, mostly by hand a series of 37 tunnels to connect the two ends of the track. The railway was not a continuous line. Spurs and branch lines were built sometimes for no apparent reason, some double, some single track. The new towns and trains were frequently attacked by bandits, ex-convicts and gold-seekers.

The world was fascinated by the achievement. In 1903/4 the first trains ran the full length of the railway and soon a regular service was established. There were three classes of carriages.

First class, blue, was used by the rich and was very luxurious.

Second class, yellow, was also comfortable but not luxurious. Rich parents travelling first class put their children and the governesses into yellow class to give themselves peace and quiet during the long journey.

Third class, green, known as 'hard' class was cheap, uncomfortable, cold, overcrowded by peasants, noisy with singing, drinking and some fighting.

At the long halts, food could be bought – every town had its speciality and hot water for tea was always available.

When war began all this changed. Supplies of military equipment and ammunition from the Entente powers, including Japan, were sent west from the Pacific coast. Prisoners of war were sent the other way to camps in Siberia. Maintenance of the railway had not been a priority and for years its condition deteriorated. Trains which broke down were simply left to rust,even on the tracks, blocking the system.

With the war in the east over the now powerful Legion was needed in France. Russia had three major ports, Murmansk, Archangel and Vladivostok. The first two in the north-west were closed in the winter and reaching either would involve a difficult journey through hostile groups. Vladivostok was a continentaway on the sea of Japan and could only be reached on the Trans-Siberian Railway, across the whole of Siberia. For the Legion it would be a daunting task to reach Vladivostok but it was the only alternative to remaining in Russia. The first priority was to move east from Ukraine where most of the Legion was located and to take control of the railway.

Marek was involved in the planning and execution of this move. He heard reports of attacks on the Legion by German army units still in Ukraine, despite the armistice. They had already entered Kiev, the capital of Ukraine and had not put down their arms. They were actually shipping grain to Germany while the local population was starving. Marek quickly gathered more information from Legionnaires and a few prisoners, recent deserters from the enemy army.

It became obvious that these attacks were not random but organised by the German leadership, keen to murder the Czech and Slovak 'traitors' who had rebelled against their country. Worse still, German units had pressed on east to establish an ambush along the railway. Marek immediately told the General what he had found out. He was shocked and ordered Marek to inform all commanders of the threat.

Bachrach Depot, lying ahead was a key junction of several lines being used by straggling Legion units which had to be secured at all costs. A major battle developed in early March 1918 when the Legion fought off German attempts to stop their progress east. From then on there were no contacts between German troops and the Legion. Legion units now controlled the whole length of the railway but they were stretched very thinly and their grasp was tenuous.

In early 1918 Trotsky agreed to allow the Legion free passage on the railway to Vladivostok in exchange for the surrender of their heavy weapons. Neither side trusted the other and when a fight broke out between soldiers of the Legion and released Polish prisoners of war, Trotsky received an exaggerated report of the incident. He rescinded his permission and informed the local soviets throughout Siberia that any Legionaires found with weapons were to be disarmed and shot. Hostilities soon erupted in towns and cities across the railway and the Legion was now reluctantly at war with the Bolshevik government.

The chaotic situation in the country continued but clear groups were emerging. Large sections of the army remained loyal to the absent Tsar. Trotsky now took charge of the Bolsheviks and raised a huge militia by conscription. At first it was just a rabble of workers in the major cities and uncoordinated groups of peasants in the countryside. It grew when soldiers returning from the battlefield joined. The units were now better led and to the concern of the Legion, the Bolshevik militia, now known as the Government's Red Army, was taking control of important towns and stretches of track along the railway.

Eventually the Legion headquarters and many trains were moved to Omsk, a city in Siberia beyond the Ural mountains. The general staff assessed the situation. There were two places that the Bolsheviks held and which they had to take – by negotiation, if possible, otherwise by force. It soon became apparent that it would have to be by force.

Further east were the crucial thirty-seven tunnels through the mountains close to Lake Baikal. Blowing up even one of the tunnels would split the Trans-Siberian Railway in two. Opening the route again would take at least two years. It was essential for the Legion to take control of the heavily fortified stronghold of Irkutsk. Colonel Gajda was surprised when the town fell to his Legion troops with little resistance. He then heard that a large contingent of Bolsheviks had slipped out of town on a train carrying a wagonload of high explosives, moving in the direction of the tunnels, and stopping at the small town of Kultuk near the entrance to the first tunnel.

The colonel took five hundred men on a three-day-and-night march across rivers and mountains. Although exhausted, at dawn on the next day they attacked the town. The defenders had not thought it necessary to post guards. They were taken completely by surprise while still asleep. The outnumbered attackers made the maximum noise, screaming and shooting at random. The guards panicked and some fled into the forest. Suddenly the wagon full of explosives was hit by a stray bullet and there was an enormous explosion. Guards were for a moment paralyzed, then they scattered. All was silent – the town no longer existed. The tunnels were saved.

At headquarters in Omsk Marek was called into the General's office. The General seemed concerned and he spoke more slowly and hesitantly than usual.

'We have to take Yekaterinburg, that is clear. It is a key rail junction just on the Siberian side of the Urals, and heavily defended by Bolshevik troops. Our colonel in charge assures me that he can take the city but I think that he is being too optimistic. He will probably need reinforcements and a lot more ammunition and food.

I want you to go to his headquarters and give me the facts and your assessment of the coming battle.'

The General had informed the leaders that Marek would be coming. On arrival he was to meet first with the staff, to be briefed on the plans. When he was shown into the major's office he was astonished. The major was none other than Stefan! They were delighted to see each other. They had not met since they had completed basic training. There was not much time for reminiscing.

Stefan very briefly related the life he had lived in the intervening years. He had become expert at planning the deployment of troops and supplying them with weapons, ammunition and food. Marek was pleased that his friend's organisational talents had been recognised and were being put to good use.

Stefan outlined plans for the attack on Yekaterinburg. The city was well defended by thousands of soldiers, heavily outnumbering the Legion attackers by about three to one. Stefan was sure that if the battle lasted for more than two days then they would need reinforcements. Marek noted all these things and then had a brief meeting with the colonel. There was no time for him to report to the General in person. Marek gave his report to be transmitted by telegraph after it was first encrypted. The General immediately gave his consent for the attack at the same time giving instructions for reinforcements to be sent along the railway line.

The Bolshevists expected the attack and the battle was hard fought over three days, moving forward and back as ground was gained and lost with heavy casualties on both sides. On the third day, Legion troops breached the outer defences of the city and entered the centre. Vicious street fighting took place but by late in the day the remaining Bolshevik soldiers fled.

Early next morning Marek, Stefan and the Colonel wandered around the town centre. The place was almost deserted and there was an eerie quiet. They spoke with a few people and discovered a secret which was about to rock the world. The Tsar and his family had been murdered in a suburb of the town.

As the Legion's attack became imminent, the local authorities sought orders from the highest level of government as to what to do with their prisoners. It is not clear from all the evidence whether Lenin gave the order to kill the royal family. Perhaps he hadn't finally decided. It is highly unlikely that it was done without his approval or at least without his prior knowledge. Time passed and the guards got no clear answer, so in the early morning of

July 17, 1918 they instructed the family to dress. Another move, the Tsar probably thought, perhaps even to England. But they were taken to the basement where the guards opened fire at random. Several of the family members died immediately while others were only injured and were beaten or bayonetted to death. The guards then spent the next two days destroying the evidence. The remains of the royal family were burnt and then thrown down a mineshaft. The authorities had thought that the Legion, backed by White formations, was coming to rescue the royal family. In fact they didn't know that they were there. So the Legion unwittingly contributed to the assassination.

Chapter Ten

Lenin had a quandary when he took power. His aim was to establish a people's paradise on his version of the principles of Marx and Engels. He knew that this could not be done immediately – indeed, it might take a generation. All traces of the aristocratic Tsarist regime, its structures and culture had first to be eliminated. This might be achievable since the returning soldiers, peasants and factory workers hated their royal oppressors. The serfs might be free but Russia was inhabited by hungry, mutinous people living like slaves.

Lenin's problem was that almost all his Bolshevik supporters were illiterate. He didn't wish to rule over a country suffering famine and disease which Russia was now rapidly becoming. He needed some educated, technically trained people. He needed some aristocrats, so he had to protect a few, while making it clear to them who was boss.

There were nearly two million aristocrats, less than two-percent of the huge population. Many were well educated, skilled in the professions of law, medicine, engineering and administration. Unfortunately they were arrogant, regarding themselves as superior and making sure that the majority underclass understood it.

The reaction of many of the aristocrats to the revolution and the abdication of the Tsar was surprising. They had grown tired of the oppressive rule of Tsar Alexander III which hadthe more liberal government of his father, Alexander II, which had included freeing the serfs. They had become frustrated by the incompetence and corruption of their present rather weak leader, Tsar Nicholas, who had never wished to become emperor and who recognised his own weaknesses for the position. So when he abdicated and the relatively moderate Kerensky took control many aristocrats adapted a 'wait and see' attitude.

As they always did, many aristocrats spent the summer of 1917 at their estates, returning to St Petersburg and Moscow in September to enjoy city life. The opera houses, concert halls and theatres were packed as usual.

Circumstances had been against Kerensky. His Provincial Government was slow to implement land reform in the countryside, famine spread and Lenin's Bolshevik militias grew in strength.

The news of the abdication took days and sometimes weeks to reach all the estates. The labourers were slow to understand the sea change in their situation. In some cases groups of peasants tentatively approached the landowners asking for half of the land and co-operation in managing it. Then extremists criss-crossed the countryside 'informing' peasants of their rights after the decades of oppression, persuading them to take over the land, ransack the houses, steal the contents, chase out the landlords and their staff, kill them if possible, and set fire to the buildings to ensure that they couldn't return.

At first there was an optimistic spirit in the air. Against all reality many aristocrats thought that the troubles in St Petersburg and Moscow would soon blow over and that they would return to their palaces and estates quite soon. It didn't happen. After the counter revolution which brought Lenin and Trotsky to power the situation of aristocrats deteriorated. They left their country estates, never to return.

In the cities they were at best tolerated, at worst demoted, insulted, turned out of their houses and beaten. Many sold their possessions for a pittance to buy food and wore red insignia to suggest that they were revolutionaries. Some who could went abroad. Others tried to get scarce rail tickets to go south to the Odessa region where life was, as yet, unchanged. They took what they could, buried larger valuables such as paintings and silverware hoping one day to return and dig up their treasures. A 'White' army was being formed and many aristocrats joined.

In the spring and summer of 1918 the war in western Europe hung in the balance. The Entente powers proposed re-opening the eastern front, even though Germany and Russia had signed a peace treaty. British War Minister Winston Churchill was enthusiastic whereas President Wilson of the United States had serious reservations.

The British sent troops and large quantities of weapons to Vladivostok and they took the train as far as Omsk. French, American and Canadian soldiers also landed but they didn't move far inland or get involved in the fighting. A small contingent of Americans came ashore at Archangel to protect the huge store of weapons they had landed.

The Japanese brought in a large contingent but they were not helpful to the Entente cause. The Japanese government had its own agenda which included territorial gains in Russian Siberia and, more importantly to them, in the neighbouring Chinese province of Manchuria. With this objective they were pleased to see and to help cause chaos in eastern Siberia.

To establish a threat to the Central Powers the troops would have to cross Siberia on the railway and then fight the rapidly growing Red Army before they could attack the Germans. This project was ill thought out and was doomed before it really began. In America Masaryk had information from the Legion and other sources about the growing strength of the Red Army and he and his close colleagues pressed government and military leaders to stop planning for the campaign.

London and Paris were keen to continue whereas President Wilson was still hesitant and he gave confusing orders to his generals in Siberia as he and his staff tried to micro-manage the movement of American troops from Washington. In fact the Entente had missed their chance. For several months after their counter-coup the Bolshevik hold on power was shaky. At one point White Army units were in sight of the spires of the churches of St Petersburg. Together with other opponents they could have defeated the Bolshevik government.

The Legion and the White Army had control of almost the whole length of the railway by early 1918. The Legion's numbers had increased with the intake of prisoners and they began to move thousands of troops to Vladivostok. They had captured hundreds of trains including heavily armoured ones. This enabled the enlarged Legion to establish a relatively well-organised administration and it became a nation within a state.

The Legion was a very unusual army. The men were almost all literate, fluent in several languages, many with university degrees and technical qualifications. There were lawyers, doctors, engineers, carpenters, butchers, tailors, postal workers and many other skilled men. This compared with the Red Army being built, where the first recruits were almost all illiterate.

The Legion had several priorities needing immediate attention apart from basic security. The Legion was very thinly spread across Siberia. The railway, its hundreds of locomotives and thousands of boxcars were in a poor state and had to be repaired. Discarded and abandoned locomotives were salvaged whenever possible and the track and bridges were repaired. The communications by telegraph had to be strengthened.

Ex-bankers managed to establish a rudimentary banking system so that soldiers could be paid and some goods and services bought in the towns and villages along the route. A daily newspaper was published containing international news, printed on a renovated discarded printing press. There was a positive spirit of innovation throughout the Legion.

Life in the boxcars was primitive, men sleeping on boards, and even in summer the nights were cold. Every effort was made to make life if not comfortable, at least bearable. Many of the trains had armoured wagons at the front and rear equipped with powerful heavy guns. Most trains contained a bakery, a kitchen and some had facilities for tailoring and boot repairs. Despite the efforts, many men lacked boots and coats.

The cutting through the forest for the railway was in many places quite narrow. Trees had been cut down on both sides of the tracks but it was still possible for bandits and Red Army units to shoot at the trains from the cover of the trees and then to disappear into the forest. Whenever it was safe to do so, men got out of their boxcars – to exercise, play soccer and even to perform music. Men from the fine concert orchestras of Vienna and Prague even put together an orchestra and plays were performed.

Legion troops made a special effort to befriend locals by trading with them and giving them presents of captured supplies. The villagers and townspeople sold them food at times when it was in short supply – most of the time. Unfortunately, Bolshevik units terrorised the local people if they knew, or only suspected, that they had traded with the Legion, murdering whole villages.

Mail was being sent up and down the line initially for the Legion but later used by civilians when a postal service was set up. The lead in this venture was taken by

Captain Novotny, a former postal official in the Habsburg empire. He and his staff designed and printed an issue of three stamps. The designs featured life in Siberia. Two small ones showed a church in Irkutsk and an armoured train. A larger, one rouble stamp depicted a soldier on sentry duty. The stamps were produced by lithography and each design was copied six times for the printing plates.

The stamp group was 'housed' in the car next to the Colonel's car in the train where Marek was based. His job required him to move up and down the line but he had always to report back to the Colonel, so he watched the progress of the team; Captain Novotny, a pretty, dark-haired young woman and three soldiers who were involved with the printing and shipment of the stamps.

There were a few wives with the Legion. Some men had been living with the wives they brought with them when they came to work in Russia before the war, whereas a few had married locally. In fact Colonel Kucera had been living with his Russian wife in Moscow for over twenty years. They had met when he had done a design and construction job for a family of minor aristocrats. She was the beautiful twenty-one year old daughter who had a very cheerful, almost playful attitude to life.

On the trains there were no such things as married quarters. Women lived in one car together. The Colonel had his own boxcar which he partitioned between an office and a private living section, so he was able to have his wife with him. The young lady, who Marek understood was the wife of an officer serving with another unit, was being sheltered by the older, Colonel's wife.

As the weeks passed Marek ate lunch often with the postal team. He tried to engage with the young lady in conversation but although polite, she seemed rather reserved. Well, everyone was going through a difficult time and she was probably worried about the safety of her husband. Her name was Ms. Vesela. After some time she began to reminisce about her life in Prague. He realised that he was attracted to this lady; that will never do, he warned himself, she is the wife of a fellow officer.

One day they were alone and she talked of her life in Prague. She became quite animated as she described her studies as an art student. She had always wanted to be an artist, influenced by her father who was curator of the largest art gallery in Prague. She spent many hours of her childhood at the gallery and visiting other galleries, even as far away as Vienna and once to Paris with her father when he was buying two French impressionist paintings for his gallery.

Some days later Marek and Ms. Vesela ventured together into Omsk. In a curious way life seemed to be going on as normal in the town. Shops were open and business was going on as if there was no civil war. They sat together in a small restaurant and talked. Towards the end of the meal Marek commented,

'You must miss your husband.'

'Yes, I do. Very much.'

'You will soon have finished the design of the stamps and you will be able to return to his train,' consoled Marek.

She was silent for almost half a minute.

'I'm sorry, I thought you knew. He was killed two years ago in an ambush by the Germans as we left Ukraine. The Colonel was his commanding officer and he and his wife brought me with them here to Omsk.'

Marek was speechless, or nearly so. All he could do was to mutter, 'I'm sorry.' They walked back to the train in silence.

It was several days before they met again in the office boxcar. Marek's thoughts were confused. At least he need no longer reproach himself for admiring Ms. Vesela – what was her first name? He had heard the colonel's wife calling her Petra. He realised that he was falling in love with her. But he couldn't somehow bring himself to tell her, fearing a rejection. A highly sensitive woman, she realised what was happening. The next time that they were alone she commented: 'I am young enough to remarry one day but the loss of my husband is too recent for me to think of such a thing. Perhaps time will heal my bereavement and by then we may all be back home. God willing.'

So Marek was clear as to where he stood. If their relationship were to develop then he would have to be patient. In the meantime there was a war to be won and the entire Legion had to be moved to the Pacific coast.

Chapter Eleven

The White armies were spread across Siberia and western Russia, north, west and south. After the death of their leader the Tsar, many became dispirited. Various Grand Dukes claimed to be the head of state and commander in chief of the White armies. At one time there were nineteen groups claiming to lead the anti-Bolshevik armies. The Legion needed their support to safeguard the railway and the Whites needed all the support they could get including from the Legion. The Entente powers, intent on opening a second eastern front, became increasingly frustrated with the bickering and they looked for someone who could lead all these groups against the Bolsheviks.

They needed a leader and settled on a relatively young Russian, Admiral Alexander Kolchak, who was known to the Americans and the British. He had been educated as a naval officer and showed signs of brilliance during his training. He had spent several years in his twenties as an arctic explorer, for which he was decorated by the Imperial Russian Geographical Society. When war broke out with the Japanese empire in late 1903, he rushed to the Pacific coast where he took charge in several artillery battles. Wounded and taken prisoner, he eventually returned to Russia and was awarded medals for bravery.

He threw his talents into designing and commanding ice-breakers in the Bering Straits. With the material he collected, Kolchak published learned articles on the subject of ice. Tsar Nicholas II was an admirer of the young naval officer and put him in charge of his programme of reorganising the Admiralty General Staff, where he helped to rebuild the Russian navy which had been destroyed by the Japanese in 1905

In the early years of the war Kolchak organised and lead dangerous mine-laying operations in the approaches to German ports, which effectively closed these ports to shipping throughout the war. At the young age of forty-one he was promoted to vice-admiral in 1916.

The 1917 February Revolution had spread to the Black Sea Fleet. Kolchak was ordered to return to St Petersburg and was asked to give evidence to the Provisional Government about the state of the armed forces, its deterioration and collapse. He advocated a hard line to restore discipline.

Some conservative groups began to speak of Kolchak as a future leader, a strong man who could save the country from anarchy. When Kerensky heard of these rumours and potential plots he ordered Kolchak to leave for America. On arrival there he was well received and was questioned by US admirals as to the situation in the Bosporus. He helped draw up plans for an American operation in the Dardanelles but these plans were never implemented.

On Kolchak's journey back to Russia he was in Japan when the Bolshevik counter-revolution took place. Being loyal to the now ousted Provisional Government, he volunteered to join the British army, which of course wished to continue the war on the eastern front.

The British sent Kolchak to the town of Harbin in Manchuria, China to take command of soldiers guarding the Chinese Eastern Railway. This line was owned by Russia and connected at the north-end with the Trans-Siberian Railway and at the south-end it ran to Vladivostok. At this time the British intended to use Harbin as a base for reopening an eastern front against the Central Powers by first overthrowing the fledging Bolshevik government. To do this, the Entente powers of Britain, America, France and Japan would have to co-operate with the White Russians and with the Czechoslovak Legion.

With a false show of reluctance, Kolchak accepted the title of 'Supreme Leader and Commander-in-Chief of all Russian Land and Sea Forces,' and established his government in Omsk. He was recognised internationally as head of state. Apart from limited military successes earlier on, the government Kolchak headed began to fall apart.

Kolchak was courageous, intensely patriotic and loyal. He was also a loner, often losing his temper, giving orders but lacking the skills to negotiate with all the parties who would have to carry them out. Unfortunately Kolchak surrounded himself with hundreds of arrogant White officers who squabbled and treated Siberians, who could have helped them, badly.

The Legion and White Army units controlled the railway so that thousands of Legionnaires travelled to Vladivostok to board ships to Europe. They were disappointed to find that there were no ships, or only military ships bringing British and American soldiers. The drive was on for a second front in the east against the Central powers. Many British troops took the trains west and to their distress, thousands of exhausted Legionnaires who had made the hazardous journey east were ordered to join them.

The Entente authorities ordered the Legion's commanding officer: 'The Czecho-Slovak Army Corps is to form the advance guard of the Allied Armies for the purpose of re-establishing an anti-German line in Russia.' The Legionnaires had to fight their way back through towns they had recently left. Thousands retraced their steps. Vladivostok town and harbour were congested with military equipment which was intended for the war in western Russia. Units of the Legion had difficulty in securing all this equipment from raids by bandits and units of the Bolshevik militia.

The Legion was ordered to take up and hold positions along both banks of the river Volga. They were spread very thinly. The Red Army became more aggressive and by late summer 1918 the balance of the civil war was changing in their favour. The commanders of the Legion and their supporters in America and Europe constantly appealed to the Entente authorities for reinforcements in order to carry on their mission, or indeed just to survive. Despite assurances of support it never came. In fact there were not enough troops anywhere near who could have fought through to relieve them and certainly not enough to attack Germany.

The Legion felt abandoned by the Entente. They felt very bitter, their discipline suffered and there were desertions. They had to retreat with heavy losses along the railway which was being attacked. Trotsky had taken over the task of expanding the Red Army and from an unruly militia of a hundred and fifty thousand he quickly built it up to a million well trained, well lead soldiers, rested, well-armed and driven by intense hatred. He also introduced an effective measure to encourage his soldiers to fight and not to desert. Before an attack he stationed units behind the front line whose job was to shoot deserters.

The Governments of the Entente countries belatedly recognised the failure of the attempt to reopen a second front in the east. Only Winston Churchill, now out of office argued for a continued offensive against the Bolsheviks. Perhaps his view was prescient: did he foresee the danger to Europe of a communist regime in the largest European country openly encouraging revolution across the world and striving to extend its empire?

By October 1918 American forces had joined the war in France which swung in favour of the Entente. Germany was forced to agree to an armistice and this was signed on November 11, 1918, ending over four years of the most brutal war the world had ever seen. Austria - Hungary's five hundred year Habsburg empire fell apart when Emperor Karl abandoned his throne without actually abdicating and the Entente powers ratified its break up. Independent states were established and on October 28, 1918 Masaryk, already head of a government in exile, was able to proclaim the new Republic of Czechoslovakia with Prague as its capital.

Hungary had lost the war and consequently some border areas were ceded to Czechoslovakia. The Hungarian leadership did not accept this loss and a border war started. The Czechs and Slovaks fought with limited men available and so the dispute lingered on. In Russia the Legionnaires celebrated the declaration. It made them more than ever determined to get home.

The telegraph service along the railway continued to function but despite the efforts of its staff it was subject to breakdown and sabotage. Largely due to Captain Novotny's energetic efforts the postal service functioned well. The design team had recently completed a rather fine series of five stamps, each in five different colours, showing scenes of the railway trains and bridges. Sheets of stamps were printed in Irkutsk on a Japanese printer renovated by an American. Sadly this new series was never issued. The design team had now done all it could so the members split up, all intending to reach the Pacific coast and find a passage on a ship home.

Colonel Kucera's confidence in Marek was growing and they talked about the situation of the Legion, the Colonel sharing details of high level discussions he had with the General. All of them were worried. The Entente powers had brought the Legion into the government headed by Kolchak but the leaders of the Legion had little confidence in him or his staff.

Colonel Kucera started to worry about the safety of his wife and Ms. Vesela. He discussed this with them and with Marek and they all agreed that if it was safe to do so the two ladies should travel to Vladivostok. This was not easy to arrange. Troop trains were packed with soldiers and refugees and there were delays on the route.

Marek came up with a solution. Legion soldiers that he commanded had stopped a short train full of fleeing aristocrats. They pleaded with the Legion soldiers for safe passage through Omsk. It was late afternoon and Marek ordered the train occupants to stay until the following day when he would review their request. He rushedback to the Colonel and they hatched a plan to get the Colonel's wife and Ms. Vesela to safety in Vladivostok. After a long discussion the two ladies reluctantly admitted that it was safer to leave than to stay.

Early the following morning, the four walked over to the aristocrats' train. They were met by an elderly man who was surprised to see them. He introduced himself as Count .... – they couldn't catch his long name. The Colonel greeted him and came to the point, speaking in Russian.

'I understand that you are heading for Vladivostok. I can give you permission to proceed and a guarantee of safe passage but on condition that you take these two ladies with you.'

The man was taken aback. 'Please come in and meet my wife the Countess and we will discuss the situation.'

Inside the boxcars were about twenty family members and the same number of people who seemed to be servants as well as an elderly orthodox priest. The cars were orderly and had been made as comfortable as possible. After rather formal introductions, the proposal was repeated. The Countess talked to Ms. Kucerova like an old friend.

'Our estate is a long way from Moscow, just east of Yekaterinburg lying not far from the railway. My son here found these carriages on a siding with what he concluded was a working locomotive. We were frightened of the Bolsheviks in the area so after a long night of talks my husband the Count concluded that we had to abandon our home, take whatever valuables we could carry and escape to the east.'

'It must have been a heart-wrenching decision to abandon your property,' sympathised Ms. Kucerova.

'Yes, indeed but what was the alternative? Probably to have it taken by the Red Army or a crowd of peasants, as happened to several other families, and lose all our possessions as well. And perhaps even our lives.'

The two ladies recognised each other as aristocrats, occasionally breaking into French, the language in which they were most comfortable.

The parties quickly came to an agreement. The Colonel would give them a letter guaranteeing their safe passage and he would telegraph Legion units on the route. Time was of the essence and they agreed to leave within an hour, just time for the ladies to pack a few things. The colonel produced a wallet full of US Dollar notes from which he gave a handful to his wife. They said good-bye. Ms. Vesela – Petra - embraced Marek, her fingers trembling.

Chapter Twelve

The days passed inside the boxcars without incident. The Count and his wife were very friendly to their
two lady 'guests', although remaining rather formal in addressing them. The Count's son, Ivan, was a man in his early forties. An engineer by training, he took an interest in the performance of the locomotive and in ensuring that there was enough wood to keep the engine moving. Although he was clearly well educated, Petra took a dislike to his rather arrogant and supercilious manner. When he began to take an interest in her she determined to keep out of his way as much as possible, which was not easy in the confined space of the boxcars.

The Countess insisted on a routine being observed. Meals were served at regular times and the servants continued to show the almost servile respect to the family which they had been trained to do back at the estate. The dozen children were given their usual lessons by the tutor and governesses who emphasised the tradition and customs of the nobility of their rapidly vanishing world.

There was also a French girl, Marie-Louise, who had been with the family as a governess before the outbreak of war. Unable to return to France, she stayed on at her job teaching the children. By now they were all fluent in French and preferred to speak it rather than Russian. Petra sat in at the back of the classes of the older children and made progress in the language. She specially enjoyed the songs which eventually she joined in singing.

Petra helped by giving art lessons to the children which they enjoyed. They had coloured pencils but no paints and quite a lot of paper of different colours. She taught concepts such as perspective and composition, portraiture and depicting scenery and houses. In the end the children were able to decorate the inside of the boxcars with their art.

The two guards got out at each station to check that the area was safe for the passengers to leave the cars and get a little exercise. On one occasion Ivan shot a reindeer and roasted it. They enjoyed meat dishes for several days. Usually the local people were friendly and happy to trade with the travellers.

They passed through the grassland called the 'steppe.' This vast area is devoid of trees but not of all vegetation. Flowers thrived, specially iris and several species of lilies as well as other plants. Further east the landscape was broken by mountains, wide swamps and bogs, and great rivers where the train slowly crossed over bridges which had been constantly repaired.

After five weeks they arrived at the large town of Irkutsk. The Count sought out the Legion authorities who were in control of the railway. It seemed that the Colonel's message had got through and they were allocated a slot to leave in three days' time. An American train was scheduled to leave just ahead of them and the commander of this train agreed that the Count's train could follow close behind and at night, when the trains stopped, the two trains could line up close to each other. This gave the Count and his passengers some security from Japanese financed bandits who would not dare to attack their 'partners' the Americans. In the meantime they enjoyed short visits to the town but in general they kept to their boxcars.

During the last week of the journey, Petra had written a long letter to Marek telling him of the life with the aristocrats. She copied this, put the original and the copy in separate envelopes. One envelope she posted to Marek from Irkutsk, the other she entrusted to the Legion commander with instructions to give it to Major Novak when he arrived. (Marek subsequently told her that he had received both copies!). There was a telegraph message from the Colonel assuring them that he and Marek were well.

The train passed through the tunnels near to Lake Baikal and rode along the precipitous section of track high above the lake. The morning sun was rising over the lake, a bright red globe. It was mid-summer so that the lake was not frozen. The water at its deepest point was dark blue, almost black.

Beyond Lake Baikal the train made steady progress on the journey east, passing through the southern edge of the great 'taiga' forest. The trees were mainly coniferous, varieties which seemed to enjoy the extreme cold such as the larch species, pines, cedars, firs, and spruces. There were also deciduous trees. In fact there are many thousands of plants that are native to Siberia. Winters in eastern Siberia are harsh, the temperatures falling to minus 70.C. There is little rain, so that the swamps and bogs of western Siberia are not found in the east. The trains were overcrowded with refugees all heading east. Most hoped for a ride on a train but others travelled on horseback, on sleighs pulled by dogs, or simply on foot. Trade and barter flourished although there was a shortage of more or less everything.

In June 1917 a Russian officer, Grigory Semenov was sent by Kerensky's Provisional Government to Siberia to form a regiment. It was never clear why they did this or what the regiment was supposed to do. Semenov was twenty-seven years old. He had shown courage in battle in the Russian army fighting the Germans. His father was a Russian Cossack from the Baikal region and his mother was a Buryat.

Once in the area east of Irkutsk he recruited a disreputable band of Mongols and Buryats with promises of gains from looting and terrorising the population of eastern Siberia along the Trans-Siberian Railway and the area of China along the China Eastern Railway. His regiment – a band of brigands - took the side of the White Army and somehow gained the patronage of the Japanese military. Perhaps they hoped that Semenov would take part in the acquisition of territory in Asia. They supplied him with money and weapons and he also stole weapons that the British were transporting to the west.

Semenov tried to build a Mongol empire to fight against the Chinese in the style of Genghis Khan from whom he claimed to be descended. He was nominally part of the White coalition headed by Admiral Kolchak. Semenov was a violent, ruthless adventurer who drank heavily. He constantly interfered with Kolchak's leadership. The Legion and the Entente generals in Asia disliked and distrusted Semenov. In fact Semenov's activities contributed to the defeat of the Whites.

Reports from Vladivostok were confusing. The inhabitants, Legionnaires, White Army deserters and others all wished to get on a ship but there were few ships available. The town appeared to be in chaos. The Count and the ladies decided that it would be better to head for Harbin in Manchuria, China which was reportedly peaceful and wait there for the Colonel and Marek. This meant leaving the Trans-Siberian Railway at Chita, which lies nine hundred kilometres/some six hundred miles east of Irkutsk and then continuing on the Chinese Eastern Railway.

This line had been built by Russians under licence from China at the time that the Trans-Siberian Railway was constructed. It led south to the town of Harbin and on to Vladivostok and reduced the distance from Chita to Vladivostok normally taken on a long loop to the north by the Trans-Siberian Railway. After the rail link was opened Harbin grew into a major town.

Despite the proximity of bandits the aristocrats' train was not attacked. They had left the forests of Siberia behind and now travelled through barren steppe country. Camels were the means of transport of the Chinese inhabitants who came out to sell and barter food to the strange, bedraggled Russians in their boxcars. By Siberian standards the journey was short and they reached Harbin without mishap.

Petra was surprised by the shops full of food and other goods, although the prices were high. The Colonel's wife spent a few of her precious dollars on essential groceries. There were many Russians, including quite a few aristocrats. Some of these people had money but most were running out of funds and selling beautiful jewellery at low prices just to stay alive. Some tried to work at menial jobs to survive. These refugees were now relatively safe but worried about the future. If they could afford to do so they would get a passage on a boat to America and settle in California. Most couldn't.

The aristocrats continued to dream while weighing up the alternatives. It would be safe to remain but their funds were running low. Perhaps one day they could return to Russia – but in their hearts they knew this to be unlikely. Many aristocrats still held to the hope that the White Army would be victorious - wishful thinking against all the news which was coming through of Red Army advances.

There was also a group of a dozen Russian Jews who had somehow made their way to Harbin. Jews had not been safe for hundreds of years in much of Europe. They had been persecuted under so-called 'pograms' under the Tsars and now in the civil war. This group kept to themselves and didn't seem to wish to have contact with other refugees.

The Countess actually found a couple of acquaintances from her home region who had made a similar journey to theirs. They had 'seen the invisible writing on the wall' and left early so that their journey took place when the White Army and the Legion were in full control of the railway – but when news from Vladivostok was troubling. So they too had opted for Harbin rather than going on to the coast. They had few illusions about going back to their estates.

It was now early September 1919. For the moment there was nothing for the ladies to do but wait.

The stress of years of fighting, poor food, inadequate medical attention was taking its toll on the Legionnaires. The Colonel, now almost fifty, was feeling his age. His service in the Legion had not been physically strenuous but had been stressful and frequently frustrating. He had joined at the beginning and his patient, pleasant but firm manner and his fluency in French had soon led to his appointment as liaison officer with the Russian Government and with the Entente diplomats.

Marek too had less energy. He lost weight, became taciturn, speaking only when he had to and avoiding company. He thought about God. If He is all powerful as the Church teaches, why did He allow this war to start and why doesn't He stop this terror? He found no answers. Marek carried out his duties, his main task being to get as many Legionnaires onto trains and to get the trains moving east. He was particularly concerned about stragglers. If they were overtaken by the Red army, they would almost certainly not survive. Either they would be shot or they would run into the forest where they would die of frostbite or famine.

Marek travelled up and down the line trying to work with the remaining railway staff and the townspeople. In general they had been co-operative but the brutal actions of Kolchak's White officers had antagonised them. Despite all these difficulties, a large number of soldiers continued to get through to the relative safety of Irkutsk, which lay just before the Lake Baikal tunnels and from there to Vladivostok. Marek and the Colonel were among the last to leave on November 12, 1919 with the Sixth Regiment of the Legion, hearing the distant gunfire of the approaching Red Army as their train slipped out of Omsk on the long trek to Irkutsk. The inhabitants of Omsk also fled, leaving the ruins of the town to the Red Army, refugees and bandits.

Many German, Austrian and Hungarian soldiers taken prisoner by the Russians in the war had been sent to camps in Siberia. They were now being repatriated by rail. Travelling from east to west their trains repeatedly caused delays to trains going in the other direction. These former prisoners of war jeered at the Legion troops but they were unarmed so that conflict was usually avoided.

Early in the war the German armies were threatening the major cities of Moscow and St Petersburg (now renamed Petrograd) so that the Russian Government decided to empty the vaults of the huge gold and silver reserves that the Tsars had accumulated in the last decades. This bullion, almost 500 tons of it, was loaded onto an armoured train and taken east to Kazan, well away from the battle frontline. The treasure consisted mainly of gold and silver bullion and coins, including large quantities of Russian roubles, American dollars, British sovereigns, French francs and several other currencies. Several millions were spent on the war effort and smaller amounts were stolen.

When Kazan was threatened by the Red Army the treasure was moved further east to Omsk and came under Kolchak's custody. When he fled Omsk with the Red Army in close pursuit, Kolchak took the treasure with him. The thirty-six heavily laden wagons slowed him down.

Knowledge of the treasure train spread across the region and attracted thieves. Some treasure may have been stolen on route by thieves or by White Army soldiers accompanying Kolchak and there were credible reports to Legion headquarters that thirteen boxes of gold were missing. It took Kolchak over a month to cover 2400 kilometres – more than 1500 miles to reach Irkutsk where he could set up his new headquarters.

From 1919 cases of so-called Spanish flu were added to the epidemic of typhus to terrorise those using the Trans-Siberian Railway as it spread along the lines. Nothing like this illness had been seen before, almost every dose leading to a rapid, unpleasant death. In fact, there was nothing Spanish about it. In the last year of the war British and French soldiers had been living in cramped conditions on farms, often close to animals, and they got ill. Authorities did not know what was going on but whatever it was it could not be allowed to undermine morale in the ranks and at home. Press reports in the Entente countries were banned but there were no restrictions on the Spanish press which published details of a relatively smaller outbreak in Spain. Hence 'Spanish flu.'

After the end of hostilities soldiers returned to their homes in France, Britain, Canada and the United States, taking the flu epidemic with them. Eventually between forty and sixty million people died worldwide.

Marek and the Colonel reached Irkutsk well ahead of Kolchak. The Colonel enquired and was assured that the aristocrats' train had gone on its way. Apparently his instructions to allow the aristocrats' train to pass had been received and respected. The people of Irkutsk were nervous but the town functioned fairly normally. But gradually a feeling of deep despair fell on the inhabitants as the Red Army approached, cutting off the line east of the town, beyond the tunnels near Lake Baikal.

Kolchak's position was now disastrous. He could have escaped but declined to do so, apparently a matter of honour to him. He was now protected by a unit of the Legion along with the treasure train. The Americans and British had left, abandoning many Legion soldiers who were effectively now surrounded.

They asked their leadership, now in Vladivostok for instructions as to what to do with the Supreme Leader and the gold. In turn, the Generals sought instructions from their governments in Europe, without a reply. The local Soviet said that he would be taken to Moscow and be put on trial. What happened next was clear but who authorised it was never established. The Legion was blamed for handing him over, but really they had no option. The local Soviet bore no ill will towards the Legion – perhaps some of them may have fought together with the *Družina* in the first years of the war. They would be quite happy to see them leave. However, they did want their heavy weapons, the treasure and the custody of Kolchak.

Kolchak was informed that he would be handed over to the Red Army at dawn. He was handed over together with Minister Papelayev and with his mistress, Anna Timirev, who refused to leave him. Kolchak's appearance had weakened but to bystanders he looked, in his full uniform, a reminder of the Admiral who once enjoyed worldwide respect.

The Government in Moscow ordered that Kolchak be put on trial in Irkutsk. This was started and lasted a week. Kolchak co-operated by answering all the prosecutor's questions and vigorously defending all his past actions. At six o'clock on the morning of February 7, 1920, Kolchak and Minister Pepelayev having been sentenced to death, were taken outside. Anna Timirev heard shots from her cabin and her shoulders shuddered: she knew what the shots meant.

The Red Army took charge of the treasure, or rather what was left of it. Rumours persisted as to what happened to it but no reliable accounting was ever made. One rumour was that the Legion had kept some bullion before handing it over. The most probable explanation is that it found its way back into the Russian central bank.

Chapter Thirteen

The White Army had disintegrated by the late summer of 1919. Soldiers deserted, some to the Red Army, others crossed into China, while a few tried to reach Vladivostok by whatever means they could. Morale among the Czech and Slovak troops fell low. They had taken losses steadily in the last year and these continued. They were tired by years of fighting and since the declaration of the new Republic of Czechoslovakia all they wanted was to go home and work for their country. The only way still remained the railway and it had to be protected.

Since Kolchak's death and the collapse of the White Army thieves and bandits were free to attack the remaining railway staff, the property and the Legion troops. Semenov's Japanese backed force was increased by 'recruitment' of recently released convicts, keen to join in the looting. The 'White Terror' and 'Red Terror' spread across Russia. Hatred lead to random killing as a sport – shooting preceded by gruesome torture. Military discipline in what was left of the White Army had completely collapsed. Throughout Russia workers and peasants had now been encouraged by Lenin to destroy the aristocrats and the richer peasants who had horded grain when the people were starving, Typhus and Spanish flu were now widespread.

The only bright spot was the work of the Red Cross and the American branch of the YMCA. Both organisations had been working in Russia since the beginning of the war and the workers were volunteers of various nationalities. They helped anyone who needed help irrespective of which army they belonged to or whether they were government employees or refugees. As a result they were respected by all sides in the civil war and rarely attacked.

Marek and the Colonel stayed on in Irkutsk as long as they could to ensure that all the Legionnaires got on trains. The local Soviet more or less kept its word: free passage in exchange for leaving the treasure train, giving up their heavy weapons and custody of Kolchak. Despite all the difficulties hundreds of trains carrying thousands of soldiers did get through to the Pacific coast.

The Colonel was not well, probably suffering from exhaustion, so he accepted that when he reached Vladivostok he would contact a doctor. He was also worried about the safety of his wife and Petra. Before reaching Chita, he instructed Marek to leave the train and find his way to Harbin and bring the two ladies to Vladivostok. So Marek happily did as he was ordered. He soon found a train and in two weeks he was in Harbin. After a couple of enquiries he found the aristocrats' train parked in a siding. The ladies were overjoyed to see him after many weeks, each greeting him with an embrace for a long moment. Their stay had been, by Siberian standards, comfortable. The question now was what to do next.

The route now lay on the Chinese railway south and then east to Vladivostok, which could be reached in about two weeks and was fairly safe. Clearly that is where the three of them should go to get a passage on a ship. But what about the Count and Countess? It was up to them and their family and servants to decide but Marek did feel some sense of responsibility for them. He sat down with the Count and came straight away to the point.

'How long do you intend to stay here and if you leave, where would you go?' he asked.

'I have been giving a great deal of thought to our predicament in the last weeks. There are several options. The most obvious one would be to go to Vladivostok and from there we could get to Canada. I have come to accept that we will never return to our home in Russia. I was sad to leave but at the time I hoped that one day I would return to the estate that my family owned for generations and that is rightfully mine. It is now clear to me that I will never see it again

I would prefer to settle with my family in a French speaking country. If we could get to Canada it should be easy to travel to Quebec and to settle there. Our funds are running low, I have sold some of our precious jewellery but I still have sufficient for the journey,' explained the Count. He went on, 'Acquaintances I have met here intend either to settle in Harbin or to travel on to Peking or Shanghai. That is possible but I'm not sure how they will survive – the Chinese may not welcome them.'

'Yes, they could do either but there are risks – perhaps no more than any other option available,' agreed Marek. 'Let's reflect on your options and speak again tomorrow,' he added.

Marek would like to have discussed the situation with the Colonel but he was certainly still on the train. A decision couldn't wait several weeks until he might be able to exchange telegraph messages. So he told the ladies of his decision and spoke again to the Count the next day.

'I will make you an offer,' stated Marek. 'If we all go on your train to Vladivostok, I will contact the Canadians and see if they can put you on one of their ships. They are accepting Legion soldiers on ships going the relatively short distance to Vancouver. The soldiers then cross Canada by train to sail to Europe. Of course I can't be sure what they will say, but I will ask them.'

The Count looked worried. 'I have talked it over with the Countess and my son. We really don't want to go back to Russia and if the Canadians won't take us all, what are we to do? So thank you for your offer, but I think it best for us to stay here for the next weeks and see what develops.'

'We could go further south into China.' After the Emperor was deposed in 1912 and Dr. Sun Yat-Sen became President a strong Marxist movement developed in China. A civil war broke out and at the same time the Japanese were threatening to take large areas in Manchuria and to set up a puppet state.

Marek now looked for a train to Vladivostok and found one that was leaving in two days' time. He agreed a price with the leader and went back to tell everyone of the arrangement. The following day he was approached by the French governess, Marie-Louise.

'I don't want to stay here, I want to go home to my family in France, to my parents, my brothers and sisters. I have been away eight years and I'm homesick. Could you take me with you to Vladivostok? There are French soldiers there leaving on French ships. I am a French citizen and I have documents to prove it. They surely will not refuse to take me with them.'

Marek hesitated a moment. He could see the logic in what she was saying and he understood that she didn't wish to be stuck in Harbin indefinitely.

'Very well, I'll take you with us. I don't know the French commanders at the port but we can find out who they are when we arrive. If it will help I can come with you to see them. You had better tell the Countess right away.'

On the day before they left, Marek had a long talk alone with the Count, clutching a glass of vodka and eyeing the Count intently. He was not well and rather depressed but determined to look after his family and the servants. He understood and accepted the French girl's wish to go her own way and he actually paid her the small outstanding salary for the last months. The Russian roubles that he gave her were almost worthless.

Taking out his safe box, he showed Marek some of the gold and jewellery that he carried. Marek had no idea of the value but he could see that many items were of the highest quality. Two of the broaches were marked 'Faberge,' the world famous jeweller to the Tsar's family. An idea occurred to him. 'Would you sell to me two or three of those rings?' he enquired.

'Yes, which ones do you want?' asked the Count. Marek looked over several and not knowing the size that he needed he selected four, two with a single diamond and two plain gold. He could always sell the surplus ones in America. He also selected a diamond broach. In a pleasant way they negotiated a fair price and the deal was done ,Marek paying with some of the few precious dollars that he had been hoarding. Uncharacteristically the Count smiled, a rare occurrence. He guessed why Marek needed the rings.

The next day, after tearful 'good-byes' Marek and the three ladies walked over to the train and got aboard. Their journey to Vladivostok was boring and uncomfortable but they made good speed and actually arrived a day before the Colonel's train which had been attacked soon after leaving Chita and had also been held up where the track had been damaged.

On arrival in Vladivostok in the morning, Marek immediately found a place for them to live and then took Marie-Louise to find the officer of the French troops who was arranging the repatriation of the force. They were lucky. As they waited a French General came out of the office, a man whom Marek had met at a meeting a year before. The General remembered Marek and stopped to speak to him in English. This is my chance, thought Marek.

'May I introduce this French lady to you,' he asked.

'Vous êtes française?' the General asked, surprised.

'Mais oui.....' and she was off in French, too fast for Marek to understand but he got the drift of it. Marie-Louise was explaining her situation and asking for his help. After a few minutes the General turned to Marek.

'If we can find a sheet of paper I will write a note to the officer concerned telling him to help this young lady get back to France,' and he went to his car and scribbled a short note in French. Marek thanked him and saluted as the General climbed into his car.

When it was handed to him the officer was clearly impressed by the note from the General. 'Be here tomorrow at ten o'clock with your luggage – only limited personal possessions, and I will see that you are taken care of. The troop ship will sail tomorrow evening,' he told Marie-Louise. 'I will explain your situation to the ship's captain.'

The next day was busy. Before the Colonel's train arrived, Marie-Louise packed, said good-bye to the other ladies, gave them her parents' address in France, and went with Marek to the French headquarters. They found the officer whom they had met the previous day, wished each other well and Marek went off to find out whether the train had arrived.

Chapter Fourteen

At mid-day the battered train edged in next to the concrete platform. The Colonel met them and insisted that they go to Legion headquarters before meeting his wife – of course, after Marek had assured him that she was well. After the collapse of Omsk and then Irkutsk the Legion headquarters had been set-up in Vladivostok. The objectives were first, to maintain some sort of law and order in the city and second, to get Legion soldiers onto ships

The General greeted them cordially and offered them tea which they gladly accepted. He inquired about their health and they assured him that they were well. Marek opened and closed his mouth, not being sure whether to tell the General that the Colonel was anything but well. The General explained the situation at some length, the ships arriving, the number of soldiers who could travel on each ship, the trains expected. Then he stopped speaking and stared at the Colonel who wasn't listening.

'Colonel, you are certainly not well. I'm not a doctor but I can see that. You must see a doctor immediately.' Then to the sergeant at the door, 'Go over to the clinic and find out if there is a doctor on duty.' It was only a short distance across the square, and the soldier came back saying that there were two doctors there and they didn't seem to be busy.

'Colonel, go with the sergeant and tell the doctor from me that he is to give you a thorough examination and come back here to me when he has a result.' The Colonel went out and Marek was left with the General.

'You will be on my staff, we need all the help we can get. Our officers are working long hours and they are exhausted. Come, we will go over to the operations room, you can meet the team and they will brief you on the situation today. We are arranging to fill a small American Navy hospital ship with the wounded, probably about three hundred. It is in the harbour and will sail in two or three days, as soon as we can get the invalid soldiers on board. But let's go back to my office to hear what the doctor has to say about the Colonel's health.'

Back after only a few minutes, the Colonel appeared with adoctor.

'Well, what is your conclusion, doctor?'

'Certainly severe exhaustion, probably other problems. He will be short of some vitamins and minerals. Like most soldiers he has not been exposed to strong sun for years and will certainly be low on vitamin D. He has lost weight. I suspect there may be other conditions – problems with kidneys or liver and I note irregularity in his heart beat. I haven't got the equipment to carry out tests of these areas,' explained the doctor.

'That doesn't sound good. Colonel, we need to get you to a hospital,' said the General. 'Doctor, where is the nearest hospital where they can do such a thorough examination and then treat him for whatever they find?'

'Oh, not in Vladivostok. Certainly in Tokyo, Vancouver or San Francisco.'

There was nearly a minute of silence. Then the General spoke.

'You might not like this, Colonel, but we could put you on the American hospital ship sailing for San Francisco in two or three days' time. How do you feel about it.' He didn't say that if the Colonel didn't agree, he would ask the doctor's opinion and if necessary, order him to go.

'If it is necessary I will go but my wife is with me and I can't just leave her here in Russia.'

'I understand that. We will have to do something about it,' replied the General.

Marek had an idea. 'The soldiers need care during the voyage. Could she travel with them to help in the nursing of the invalids?'

'That might be possible. The Red Cross will probably send two or three nurses which will be inadequate. They are very short staffed. Several have succumbed to typhus and others have sailed home. I suggest that you go and talk to them. You had better go now as there is no time to lose,' concluded the General and he thanked the doctor and showed them all out.

It was late in the day and the Colonel wanted to see his wife and to rest. They found the two ladies, had a light meal and then talked about their situation. Mrs. Kucerova was also shocked to see how ill her husband looked. She accepted that he had to go on the hospital ship but she flatly refused to stay behind without him. And if she was going then she would take Petra with her.

The next morning the Colonel rested while the two hoping-to-be nurses and Marek found the office of the Red Cross. It was staffed by Americans. They introduced themselves to a lady who said that she was the senior nurse and they explained their difficulty. Marek spoke in English since she understood little Russian. She listened carefully.

'I'm sorry but the Red Cross can't just accept anyone without medical qualifications and allow them to wear a Red Cross uniform. They might get away with this in an emergency in a battle zone but the ship would certainly fly the American flag and American law would apply on board. They would be strict about following their regulations. I have to contact the officers of the ship to confirm whether they need our nurses.'

'Well, I understand your predicament,' she continued. 'Frankly if I were you, and don't quote me on this, I would simply find a way to get aboard and lie low until the ship has sailed. Then you can offer to co-operate in looking after the welfare of the invalids. Your work doesn't have to be of a medical nature. Morale of the soldiers is paramount. You will perform a great service if you just listen to them talking in their own language and encourage them. The American medical staff will surely appreciate this; and if they don't, there would be nothing they could do about it – they can hardly throw you overboard.' Marek laughed. He quickly translated into Czech. 'Sorry that I can't be more helpful. Good luck,' she wished them as she showed them out.

The list of soldiers, their name, date of birth and a brief five to ten word description of their ailment was being completed by Legion staff to be given to the Captain of the ship which had now arrived in the harbour. Colonel Kucera was listed with the ailment 'intense fatigue' and there was a note from the doctor recommending urgent tests for various conditions with Latin names and (to a layman) meaningless abbreviations. The three hundred and twenty four invalids were to embark the following morning and the ship would sail before sunset.

Marek was helping to complete the list and checking it as far as possible. For a few severe cases, a doctor's report was attached. By eight o'clock in the evening he was satisfied that it was correct – that is, as 'correct' as he could make it on the information that was available. He stood up, paced up and down for a few minutes in the deserted office and then sat down. At the end of the list, he added two names, J. Kucerova and P. Vesela, describing them as 'support staff.' At least he reflected, they will not be charged with having boarded illegally, as stowaways.

At noon the next day the invalid soldiers began to board the hospital ship. First those who had to be carried aboard on stretchers, then the 'walking wounded.' All this took several hours as each soldier had to be identified, checked with the list and a tag attached to his wrist. Ms. Kucerova and Ms. Vesela helped with moving the invalids aboard.

The process was finished only a few minutes before the ship was due to sail at eighteen hundred hours. Marek handed the list to the First officer, a Lieutenant Commander, saluted and went ashore. He looked out at the grey mist and watched as the ship slipped quietly out of the harbour into the dark Pacific ocean to begin the long voyage of eleven thousand, five hundred kilometres/seven thousand miles to San Francisco.

The First Officer sat down to review several matters with the head nurse, Lieutenant Johnson. Arrangements would have to be made for any special diets and the head cook informed. Urgent cases would have to be reviewed this evening. He went down the list until he came at the end to two passengers listed as 'support staff.'

'Who are these two men and what are they supposed to support?' he asked. A Czech speaker would immediately have recognised that the two names were names of married women.'Find them and bring them here,' he ordered a sailor. This took some time but eventually the sailor returned and apologised for taking so long. 'The two men are ladies,' he blurted out.

'What? What are you talking about?Men can't be ladies!'

'Commander, they are here, outside your cabin.'

'Well, bring them in,' the officer ordered.

The two ladies entered, to the astonishment of the First Officer and nurse Lieutenant Johnson.

'And to what do I owe the pleasure of your company,' he enquired sardonically.

Petra explained as best she could in her limited English that they were aboard to help the soldiers in any way they could.

'We have two doctors and ten nurses to do that,' replied the First Officer.

'Yes, but we speak their language. We can even help explaining their problems and make them feel better.'

'All right, you are here so perhaps you can make yourselves useful. If I had known about you this afternoon, I would not have taken you. I can't say, 'Welcome aboard'.'

'When we have finished our work Lieutenant Johnson will take you to the nurses' quarters, you can sleep there. For the voyage you will be under the authority of the Lieutenant. Is that clear?'

'Yes, quite clear,' replied Petra, and they went outside to wait.

'Well, it could have been worse,' commented Petra as she translated what had been said.

In the next days and weeks they spent their time with the soldiers, listening to their stories, conveying their requests to the nurses. Each day they had a few minutes with the Colonel. He was quite contented, relaxing with a book and talking to the other soldiers. They were now no longer on active service so he never emphasised his rank, although it was obvious to them that he was a senior officer. Like his wife and Petra, he was able to encourage the soldiers about their plans for the future 'back home' and to give the younger ones some advice. They respected and liked him as a father figure. It was impossible to spend much time on deck because the movement of the ship created a cold breeze all the time.

After a month they arrived in the harbour of San Francisco. Before disembarking they said 'Good Bye' to the nurses who had all been friendly and some of the soldiers. They had not seen the Lieutenant Commander since their first conversation but he now made a point of speaking to them, thanking them for their work and wishing them a good onward journey.

Chapter Fifteen

Disembarking the soldiers took several hours. Some were able to walk and some were carried on stretchers. They were taken to a military hospital for more thorough examination. Most were released after a few hours, including the Colonel. The diagnosis was of severe fatigue but the results of some tests would only be available in a few days so he was given an appointment in one week. In the meantime he was advised to rest, walk a little, sit in the sun each day but not for too long and relax as much as possible. His wife and Petra went to meet him at the hospital. Leaving, they were approached by a young couple. The young woman spoke to them in halting Czech.

'We are members of the San Francisco branch of the Czech and Slovak Association. Your soldiers are all heroes to us. If we can help you in any way, please tell us how. Have you anywhere to stay?'

'No, we need to find somewhere for at least a week, perhaps longer,' replied Petra.

'If you need a hotel we can recommend one. A cheaper alternative would be to stay in a student hostel which is open to visitors while the students are away on the summer vacation. The rooms are very nice and you can make tea and even cook small meals. We could take you to see them if you would like,' they offered.

The Colonel had doubts about staying in a student place but they decided that they might as well see the rooms.

'Yes, can you tell us how to get there?' asked Petra.

'We have a car parked across the road and it will take only about ten minutes,' the lady assured them. 'It's near the university campus.' The car was a Ford Model T, one of the millions being produced on the Ford production line. It was painted black, following Henry Ford's offer that that 'you can have any colour that you like as long as it's black.'

The five of them crammed into the car for the short journey. When they got to the building there was an office dealing with summer rentals of rooms to vacationers, so they were shown one. It was not large but nicely decorated and clean. There were two single beds, a shower room and a small mini - kitchen in the corner. The price was very reasonable compared to what they would have to pay in even a modest hotel. Since they didn't have an alternative they agreed to take two rooms for two weeks. The agreement made, the young couple invited them to a drink of tea or coffee.

'We know a nice place by the beach only a short drive away.' It was a simple beachside café offering drinks and ice-cream and there was a view of the sea, the waves lapping gently on the golden sand.

The host lady talked a lot, in a mixture of Czech and English. 'My name is Lucie and my boyfriend is Elmer. We are studying for masters degrees at the University of California here in San Francisco. It is his hometown and I'm from New York. I'm here during the vacation because I'm attending a special seminar on my subject, marine biology, in which the University is a world leader. Elmer is learning about Economics, which must be terribly boring.'

In response to Lucie's questions, Petra explained who they were and that she was waiting in San Francisco for her friend, Major Marek Novak who must soon arrive on a ship. Lucie respected the sensitivity of the situation and asked no more questions. She figured that Petra would tell her the story when she was ready.

Ten days later the next ship arrived from Russia and to Petra's disappointment, Marek was not onboard. This did not surprise the Colonel as he knew that Marek would stay as long as he was needed. The soldiers came onshore. The special train to New York left the following day. The Colonel was considered by the doctors to be well enough to travel and he and his wife said good-bye to Petra at the station, promising to meet her again in Prague.

Petra was now alone in San Francisco. In the days and weeks that followed, Lucie and Elmer took her under their wings. They introduced her to other first and second generation Czechs and Slovaks. There was an office of the Legion which was working with the city authorities to receive soldiers from the ships, give them decent clothes which the public had donated in huge quantities, help organise medical checks, arrange a stay of one or two nights before seeing them onto trains bound for New York.

Many soldiers wrote letters home, proudly addressing the envelopes to 'Republic of Czechoslovakia,' the country they had never known in its new form. Lucie and her American friends in the office added postage stamps and mailed the letters. Petra wrote several, all to her parents with messages for family and friends. She didn't mention Marek, perhaps not knowing what to write. She mailed the letter that Marek had given her addressed to his parents.

Petra helped with the tasks whenever a ship arrived, which was now roughly once a month. There was a frantic forty-eight hours, the train would leave and then all was quiet again. She could help with the few special cases of soldiers who couldn't travel. She visited them in hospital and tried to respond to their requests.

Lucie introduced her to other students. There seemed to be a group of a dozen who were close friends, having come through their years as undergraduates and who were now studying for masters degrees. Petra enjoyed their company but much of the time she was alone, taking long walks on the beach, walking barefoot in the shallow waves.

The previous week Petra had passed a photographer's shop and had gone in to get six small photos which she would certainly need for documents. At the back of the shop was a large room marked 'Gallery Open' so she went in. The photographer had enlarged and framed about thirty photographs which were clearly taken in San Francisco and the Bay area. The photographer came in to join her, and apparently having few customers, he spent half an hour describing the photographs. They were taken on Sundays and public holidays when the shop was closed and he had time for the hobby side of his activities.

The photographershowed her his three cameras and described his outlook on landscape and portrait photography. He expressed the view that photographs could be artistic and Petra agreed. She thought that photography could fit in well with her activities as an artist. Back in Prague she did not intend to confine herself to traditional women's activities - to the three German K's - '*Kinder, Kuche, Kirche,*' but to use her artistic talents for her enjoyment and to earn money.

Petra went over and over one subject in her mind. She was fairly sure that Marek, when he arrived would soon propose marriage. She needed to be clear in her mind about her response. Almost four years had passed since Filip's death, but he was still fresh in her mind. If he could see her, would he mind if she re-married? She didn't think that he would. And Marek, he could never really replace Filip. No one could.

Marek was a kind man, decisive, quiet, handsome in a way, interested in some of the things that interested her, such as art and music – though he didn't seem to know much about art. If they had children he would surely be a good father and would certainly work hard to support his family. Perhaps she didn't know how he would behave in peacetime. To know someone, one needs to see him or her in different life circumstances, she reflected. How would Marek behave when surrounded by his own family? Would he be respectful to his parents and grandparents? Such opportunities were not available to her. She had only seen him at war. He would certainly become less taciturn when the stress of war was removed from his life.

If they married she was sure that she could come to love him over the months and years. She made up her mind. She would say 'Yes.'

Students were drifting back and the fall semester would soon start in the universities. Lucie dropped-in to invite Petra to join the 'gang' at a student dance on Saturday evening. She had met and liked a few members of Lucie's 'gang,' others would be there so she accepted. They met at the dance hall, took over a big table with a dozen chairs and ordered bottles of the local wine. The band started to play and gradually the floor filled with dancers. Several couples from her group got up, including Lucie and Elmer, and she was left alone at her end of the table.

A man called Bill asked her to dance. Tall, handsome, with ginger hair he looked to be about eighteen, but with an undergraduate degree and now on a masters course he must be at least twenty three, perhaps older. Petra had danced a lot in her student days back in Prague and with Filip in Moscow but these dances were completely strange to her. No polkas or mazurkas, or set piece dances, not even a Viennese waltz. Couples held each other and some girls danced alone!

When she apologised for her ignorance of the steps Bill brushed her remarks aside and led her through the dances, which he called the foxtrot and the tango. This he explained was from Argentina. They went out onto the large terrace and he walked her through the steps. He was clearly a good dancer. Returning to the dance hall she began to enjoy learning these, to her, strange American dances. They took a break to sit down and drink some more wine. The rest of the 'gang' were dancing so that they sat alone, in silence as conversation was impossible against the music. Then back to the dance floor.

As the evening passed, Bill gradually held her more tightly as they danced and then stood with his right arm around her waist between the numbers. Petra became tired and slightly dizzy so to get some air she suggested that they go out onto the terrace. It was deserted. Bill continued to hold her in an embrace and soon began to kiss her. She let him do so. 'What am I doing'? thought Petra. But she didn't stop him until the band struck up 'Auld Lang Syne,' the dancing ended and they went inside to the table.

The others were leaving in little groups. Lucie and Elmer had already left. Dark clouds hovered as moonlight barely shone along the cloud's edge. Bill offered to take her home. Her apartment was only about ten minutes' walk away but some of the students had been drinking heavily and she decided that it would be safer if he accompanied her. Stepping onto the path she realised how exhausted she was. After a few minutes Bill stopped.

'My apartment is here, in this building. Would you like to come in? I can make a cup of coffee and you can rest a little,' he offered.

'Thank you, but it's late and I'm tired, so I would prefer to go to my apartment,' she replied.

'Okay, good night,' and he took her in his arms and kissed her more passionately than he had done on the terrace. She let him do so, becoming dizzy. Perhaps he sensed this. He picked her up, slung her over his shoulder and carried her up to his apartment.

The sun was streaming in through the window when they woke on Sunday morning.

'I'll make coffee and toast,' said Bill.

Petra got up, found a towel and went into the shower. As she dressed, she noticed several ladies' dresses hanging in the cupboard.

They drank the coffee and ate the toast in silence. He had a self-satisfied smirk on his face. 'Like the cat that had found a bowl of cream left on the kitchen table and licked it all up,' thought Petra. She was shocked and ashamed at what they had done. But she was most ashamed that she had actually enjoyed it.

She slipped out, walked the short distance home, lay down and fell asleep. In the afternoon she decided to go for a walk. She had no idea what time it was. Where was her watch? It was nowhere to be found. Then she realised that she had not picked it up when she had dressed. It must be somewhere in Bill's apartment. There was nothing for it but to go and collect it.

She walked over there and knocked several times on the door but no-one answered. She would come back tomorrow. So she walked round by the main university buildings. The clock on the tower showed five-thirty. She really must get her watch back tomorrow.

At lunch time on Monday she knocked on Bill's door and he answered.

'Well, hello, what can I do for you'? he asked with his usual smile.

'I left my watch here,' Petra explained.

'I haven't seen it, but do come in and we can look for it,' he offered.

As soon as she entered the apartment she remembered that she had put it on the bedside table but it wasn't there. It must be on the floor somewhere, so she went down on her knees and in a few seconds found it.

Bill helped her to her feet and made a move to embrace her. 'No!,' she said very firmly and he backed off. 'I hope you won't tell anyone,' she implored, worried at the possibility that he might start bragging.

'Don't worry, your guilty little secret is safe with me,' he assured her. Unknown to Petra, his live-in girlfriend was returning from vacation later in the week so he had certainly no intention of showing off about his exploits.

The next days were filled with turmoil in Petra's emotions. She enquired at the Legion office as to when the next ship would arrive. It seemed that most of the Legion soldiers who had reached Vladivostok had been transferred to America or Canada, while other ships had taken the longer route across the Indian Ocean to Europe. Now the last few ships were going to Vancouver in British Columbia, Canada, and only one more was expected in San Francisco in about ten days' time. Surely Marek would be aboard that one. She was terrified at the thought that she might be pregnant. Now she had just to wait for Marek to arrive and for confirmation in about ten days' time that she was not pregnant. She could easily remember the date of last Saturday – it had been her thirtieth birthday.

Chapter Sixteen

The Trans-Siberian Railway had been occupied in several places by the Red Army as Legion units headed for the coast. No more trains were arriving in Vladivostok, communications had broken down completely so that it was impossible to know how many stragglers there might be. The future for them was bleak. The Red Army would certainly shoot them. In the forest they would soon die of hunger or the cold. A few might make it across the border to China or Mongolia where the chances of survival might be better. The same thing would be happening to the remnants of the White Army, officers and soldiers. Some of the soldiers might join the Red Army

American, British and French troops had left on military ships and only the Japanese remained. In fact, more were still arriving. They moved out of the city to an area which their government had taken over to the north. Clearly the Japanese government was pursuing territorial ambitions on Russian Siberia and Chinese Manchuria.

The town of Vladivostok was falling into chaos. Starving groups of refugees were stealing supplies and setting fire to buildings. Legion soldiers were able to hold the harbour area for ships to dock. Before leaving, many soldiers raided the abandoned stores so that they were quite well dressed as they boarded the ships.

Marek had been working on lists, long lists of soldiers who would board each ship. There was also an incomplete list of Legionnaires who had been killed. The name of Lt. Vesely was there, with the date 1916. Glancing through the lengthy list he was shocked and deeply saddened to read 'Major S. Dvorak, 1918.' This must have been soon after they had worked together on the battle for Yekaterinburg. Marek made a mental note that when he got home he would seek out and visit Stefan's family.

There was nothing more for Marek to do so he boarded the last ship for San Francisco. It was overcrowded and the voyage was long and uneventful.

At the harbour Petra raised her hands above her eyes looking for the ship, anxiously waiting for it to dock. She was delighted to meet Captain Novotny, who was also waiting for the ship to arrive. He told her that he had come to San Francisco on an earlier ship and had brought with him hundreds of large sheets of the unissued stamps which she had helped to design. He was arranging with the American authorities and the recently opened Czechoslovak Embassy in Washington D.C. to have the stamps shipped to the Post Office in Prague. The arrangements were now complete so he intended to take the train which would carry the newly arrived soldiers to New York.

The ship arrived and Marek came ashore to be greeted with a warm embrace from Petra. He looked tired but he had rested during the long voyage and with no responsibilities he had finally been able to relax. Petra had reserved an additional room for him at the small hotel which she had moved to when the students had all returned, so they walked over to it. They discussed plans for the journey home. The special train to New York would leave the next day or the morning of the following day and this would be the last one. If they didn't take it they would have to buy tickets for a later train and this would exhaust their funds, which were anyway running low.

Petra took Marek to the photographer to get a few small photographs which he would soon need. In the afternoon, Elmer called at the hotel and took them on a tour of San Francisco, as Petra had been taken when she had arrived. Marek was amazed at the affluence of America. They joined Lucie at a tea shop on the hill overlooking the city. She was so pleased to meet Marek.

She explained that she had exchanged letters with her mother and her parents were very keen to meet a hero of the Legion and they hoped that Petra and Marek would stay with them in their home at White Plains, a small town to the north of New York City. Her parents would meet them off the train. Elmer sensed that Marek and Petra wished to be alone, so they kept their good-byes for the next day when they would come to see them off. Petra knew of a pleasant restaurant for dinner, where Marek enjoyed an enormous steak. It was a mild evening so they walked to the beach. Sitting on a bench, Marek haltingly popped the question.

'That's lovely of you to ask me. I'm sorry but I really need to think it over for a few days. It's such an important decision to get right. Just give me a little more time,' she replied.

Slightly disappointed but not depressed, after all it was not a refusal, Marek kept the two diamond rings in his pocket. They went to the hotel and both slept well. When Petra woke early in the morning she was relieved to find that she was not pregnant. With the threat gone she could now happily accept Marek's proposal of marriage.

The train was leaving the next morning. They went clothes shopping for Marek and then to a fish restaurant. As they finished their meal and other diners had left, Petra leaned over the table and whispered 'Yes,' gave him a big smile and a gentle kiss. As was his nature, he said little, the emotion was too great. Tears rolled down his cheeks as he produced one of the diamond rings. It fitted perfectly; the other one would have been too small and it could be sold before they left America.

Their friends were at the station to see them off. Petra showed them her ring and they were delighted at the news.

'You really must meet my parents. I will give them a telephone call this evening and tell them of your engagement,' said Lucie.

It was soon time to find their seats. They hugged, wished each other farewell and promised that they would meet again.

When the trains for soldiers had begun to run, railway company officials were embarrassed to be sending exhausted soldiers in third class coaches. They need not have worried. The soldiers thought they were travelling in luxury! The seats were upholstered and they folded down at night to make a bench to sleep on. Marek had the same reaction.

They were served a substantial meal before the Union Pacific train ran through superb scenery, mountains, forests, rivers, but which was impossible to enjoy after nightfall. The first stop was at Salt Lake City, capital of the state of Utah. Thousands came out to welcome the heroes that they had read about in newspapers for four or five years. Throughout the war several intrepid American journalists had followed the Legion and had filed stories about them so that the public had followed their fortunes. The people brought a lot of food, mainly home cooked and doughnuts, doughnuts and more doughnuts! It was the same in Chicago, where the train stopped for two hours to take on provisions. Against regulations someone had given the soldiers a large crate of beer. They had a riotous party on the last leg of the journey, singing old Czech and Slovak songs all night long.

After a journey of three days and nights the train pulled into Grand Central station, New York at ten o'clock on a beautiful Sunday morning.. The soldiers were treated like royalty, brass bands played Czech and Slovak music and thousands of first and second generation Czech and Slovak Americans were in the cheering crowd.

Chapter Seventeen

Lucie's parents were at the station, carrying a banner saying, 'Welcome to Major Novak and his Wife.' Petra was the first to spot the banner and she remarked to Marek that this greeting would have to be corrected! Lucie's parents greeted them like long-lost children. 'Major Novak, my wife and I are so honoured to meet a hero of the Legion,' said Mr. Bridges. His car was parked nearby and all four got in, Marek sitting next to him. He was especially proud of his car, a Buick painted in dark blue. It was only a year old. He explained how he enjoyed driving on Sunday when his chauffer had the day off. The roof was down allowing them all to enjoy the warm breeze.

They arrived at the Bridges' home in West Plains, a small town not far from New York City. The house stood in a large garden. It was very big, with six bedrooms and several reception rooms. Ms. Bridges showed them to their room, which was furnished with a large double bed. Petra immediately spoke up.

'I think there has been a misunderstanding. We are only engaged, not yet married,' she explained.

'Oh, I thought Lucie told me that you were married last week. It was a poor line so perhaps I didn't get her message right. No problem, we will find another room for the Major,' Ms. Bridges replied. 'It is rather smaller than this one.' Marek was taken there and when he saw it he thought that it was not small - well, not as big as the double room but perfectly nice and equally well furnished.

'Have a wash, a shower or bath if you wish. Lunch will be served in half an hour.'

In the late fall it was still warm enough at mid-day to sit outside on the terrace. Lunch was served by an elderly lady, apparently a maid. The visitors were introduced to her, Ms. Bridges explaining that she had been with them for nearly thirty years and had looked after Lucie and her brother from the time they were born until they left for university.

As well as talking a lot, Ms. Bridges asked a lot of questions. However, when the subject concerned the war in Russia, she quickly noticed that her visitors were uncomfortable with the conversation. Changing to ask about their childhood and youth in what was now Czechoslovakia, Petra was happy to reply to all her questions. Lunch over, Ms. Bridges took Petra off to show her the kitchen which she was very proud of and where she spent several hours of the day.

Mr. Bridges was now able to talk. He reminisced about his life in the 1860s, just before the outbreak of the civil war and his career.

'I was born in the neighbouring state of New Jersey. Both my parents had been school teachers. Fortunately my father didn't have to fight in the civil war. Sadly, they are no longer with us. I was lucky to be admitted to study at the local university, Princeton, for my undergraduate degree in Economics. Then I moved to New York and completed a masters degree in Finance. Not surprisingly that led me to a job on Wall Street. I was fortunate to get a junior position at the age of 25 with a brokerage firm, Greenstone and Company. Mr. Greenstone was a Jewish immigrant from Germany called Herr Grünstein, a name that he soon anglicised. He ran the company alone – who the 'and Company' were could have been me and several other junior, underpaid clerks. Our hard work paid off, at least for Mr. Greenstone.'

'In his sixties his health was failing. He worked less and I, as the senior clerk, worked more. He retired and sold me the business at what I thought was a very low price. When I went over the accounts with the treasurer, he commented that the balance sheet looked 'fragile.' In fact, Mr. Greenstone had taken out all the reserves developed over two decades. As the treasurer went on to point out, 'The business is quite profitable. If you can hold on to most of the clients, and you have known them for years, and if you can keep costs down, then you can do very well.' '

'That was how things developed. In fact, I managed to expand the business and now I have over twenty staff.'

'That is a great achievement,' said Marek. 'May I ask how you and Ms. Bridges met?'

'Oh, that was in 1885. Her father was from Prague, landing here at the age of 21, he soon married a Czech girl who he met here at the Czech society. He had trained as a draughtsman and got a job in an architect's office in New York. He noticed how much money their clients were making in house sales, so taking his savings and some money he had borrowed, he started buying and selling property. Soon he had a very successful business. He built this house and left it to my wife when he died a few years ago.'

'How are your parents?' enquired Mr. Bridges.

'I don't know. I have written to them several times but I have no news of them.'

'We could try to get a telegram to them,' Mr. Bridges suggested. Marek replied, 'I have heard that communications are still unreliable outside the cities. It might be best to send it to someone who has a telephone. My parents live in a small town and I am not sure that a telegram would reach them. I don't believe that one would be delivered to Petra's parents either. When we left her father was the curator of a large art gallery, though whether he is still there we have no idea. But I have a suggestion. My father works in a large shoe manufacturing factory and he is friendly with the owner, Tomas Bata, so perhaps we could send it to him quoting his telephone number. But I don't know it,' Marek explained.

'Is that Tomas Bata of Bata Shoe Company? They recently opened a shop in New York so they will certainly have his address and telephone number. You can draft a short message and I will ask my secretary to send it. He is very reliable in such matters. The office is closed to-day, Sunday, so let's do that to-morrow. We can take a walk around White Plains and you can see what a rural American town looks like.'

They all went for a walk. Marek discovered that there were many fine houses like that of the Bridges, some larger. Petra had seen some of the houses in the San Francisco area but Marek was surprised at the obvious wealth of the town. He noticed that the gardens had no walls or fences, each merging into the neighbour's property in such a way that you couldn't tell where each property began and ended.

Back at the house they enjoyed a light supper, a delicious salmon salad prepared and served by Ms. Bridges. The visitors were tired and asked to be excused to sleep early.

Breakfast was served at eight o'clock and at half past eight Mr. Bridges suggested:

'If you wish you can come with me to my office in Manhattan. Alec, the driver, will take us and he can drive you around town to show you the sights. Then we can meet at my office and we'll all come home together.'

'That would be great,' Petra and Marek said almost together, and they hurried to get ready. The drive into town was uneventful and Mr. Bridges got out at his office which was located just off Wall Street. The driver knew the city well. He asked them what they would like to see and they replied that they had not heard of any place specially worth visiting.

'Just show us everything,' said Marek.

'For that we would need a year, not a day,' replied Alec.

'We would like to visit some shops. I have heard of Tiffany, it would be interesting to walk round it even if we don't buy anything. Marek's watch is broken so he might find another one?,' asked Petra.

'Ok, let's go,' and they drove round New York for nearly two hours. Then they walked down Fifth Avenue, wandered around Tiffany and were amazed at the quality of the products and the prices. Marek bought a cheap watch from a street seller. In another street, Marek spotted a sign 'Gold and Jewellery bought and sold.' They went in and Marek produced the two, now spare rings and the broach which he had bought from the Count.

'How much you pay me for these?' he asked the elderly man. After examining them with a microscope, he said:

'I can give you one hundred and twenty dollars,' the man offered. Marek looked at Alec, who now spoke for him.

'We have to think about it for an hour or two. We'll come back if we want to accept your offer.'

Outside the shop, Alec explained that it was best to ask in one or two other shops. He walked over to a taxi which was parked nearby and spoke with the driver.

'He has given me two addresses of places which buy jewellery, so let's try them.'

The discussion at each of the other two was almost identical to that in the first shop, except that the offers were a hundred and ten and eighty five. So they returned to the first shop and carried out the transaction. With a small part of the funds they bought a ring for Marek. By now it was time for lunch. Alec said he knew of a good place – in fact, Mr. Bridges had told him to take them there and to pay the bill. The food was excellent and the service, as always in America it seemed, was friendly and efficient. In the afternoon they walked through Central Park to the Metropolitan Museum of Art – the 'Met' to New Yorkers. It was enormous. They had seen only a small part of the collection when it was time to find the car, pick-up Mr. Bridges at his office and drive home.

The evening meal was a light one, a chicken salad, and after eating Mr. Bridges wished to talk with them.

'I have several suggestions. The last boat to Europe for Legion soldiers leaves tomorrow evening. It will surely be crowded and uncomfortable. I suggest that you don't go on it. My secretary made some inquiries today and he found that there is a ship of the Cunard passenger line, the RMS Mauretania leaving next Sunday for Southampton in England. It would be a pleasure and an honour for Ms. Bridges and me to offer this voyage to you. It will be a second class cabin rather than the formal, rather stuffy first class and better than third class 'steerage' on the lowest deck of the ship.'

'That would be extremely generous. It would be embarrassing for us to accept such a big gift,' replied Marek.

'Then you will just have to be embarrassed,' responded Mr. Bridges with a smile at his own joke.

'Well, that's settled,' continued Mr. Bridges, 'there is another matter that my wife has been concerned about.'

'Yes,' said Ms. Bridges, who so far had been uncharacteristically silent. 'You two behave as if you were already an old married couple. If you marry here then the voyage home could be a lovely honeymoon.'

This time Petra and Marek were really taken aback. Mr. Bridges took over:

'The ceremony can be performed by a judge, such as my friend Judge Benson who lives in White Plains. I took the liberty of speaking to him by telephone to confirm my understanding of the law and to ask him whether he would be prepared to conduct such a ceremony for a hero of the Legion and he agreed. So there is the offer – it could be Saturday, at the end of this week. The ship sails on the following day, Sunday afternoon.'

Petra and Marek were speechless. Eventually Petra said,

'Marek and I need to talk all this over.'

'Of course, but don't hesitate too long, bookings must be confirmed,' concluded Mr. Bridges.

Marek and Petra sat in silence in another room. It was a long time before Petra spoke.

'The voyage would be an incredible gift. Can we accept? I don't see how we can refuse - they would be very hurt if we did so.'

Another silence. 'What about the wedding? How do you feel about it?' asked Petra. 'We have only been engaged for a week!'

Marek was enthusiastic. Perhaps he was worried in the back of his mind that she would have second thoughts. 'It's all right by me,' he said.

'By me too,' responded Petra, and they hugged each other. 'Well, that's settled,' she added. 'We can tell them at breakfast. I'm ready to sleep.'

'Good, that's agreed' said Mr. Bridges as they finished breakfast. 'I'll confirm the passage with Cunard. I'll also speak to Judge Benson who lives in White Plains. I've met him often at charity functions. He is authorised to conduct civil weddings. You will have to get a licence to enable him to marry you. I've checked that with him. Alec is already here and waiting for me in the car. I'll see you all this evening.'

Ms. Bridges and Petra spent most of the day working on plans for the wedding. Petra wished to have a small ceremony, just the Bridges. Lucie's elder brother and his wife would come from New Jersey, probably bringing their two year-old son. It would be on Saturday morning at the Judge's house and they would all come back home for lunch.

That evening, Mr. Bridges walked over to see Judge Benson, who agreed to the arrangements. He confirmed that there was no residence requirement to be married in New York state. Next day, Ms. Bridges went with Marek and Petra to get the marriage licence. The officer went through their papers. Neither had the customary birth certificate which was necessary to establish that they were twenty-one years old.

'Are you twenty-one years old?' he asked them with a smile. They all laughed.

To establish his identity, Marek showed his military papers, and confirmed that he was not married to someone else. For Petra it was a bit more complicated. However, she had carefully kept her marriage certificate and the letter signed by the general informing her of Filip's death. These document were not the usual ones required but the officer accepted them, gave the licence to Marek and wished them well.

Mr. Bridges had a surprise for the others – tickets for a concert on Friday evening by the New York Philharmonic Orchestra. It was to be a special treat. The programme included the Czech composer, Dvorak's New World Symphony, written by him in America. It was based on native American music and spirituals, and reminded Marek and Petra, as it had the composer, of their longing for their home country. The concert also included a piano Polonaise by Chopin.

The week passed quickly. Alec drove them all to pick up Mr. Bridges at his office and they went to his club for a meal before walking over to the concert hall. The orchestra was conducted by a Czech, Josef Stransky who had worked in Berlin before emigrating to America. His conducting style was controversial but Petra enjoyed the music and at the end tears gently rolled down her cheeks.

Saturday dawned with a cloudless sky on a cool, late fall day. They walked over to Judge Benson's house where he was waiting, wearing his formal robes of office. The ceremony was rather simple since he had already prepared the marriage certificate. He made a short speech, asked them each whether they accepted the other, then pronounced them 'man and wife' and invited them to exchange rings and a kiss. The few people present clapped, and congratulated the newlywed couple. Judge Benson's wife had prepared snacks in the dining room and a waiter served champagne.

Returning to the Bridges' home they sat down to a delicious five-course lunch which went on to four o'clock. No-one could eat supper, so after a short walk around the town, Petra and Marek decided on an early night. They would have to leave early next morning so they decided to sleep in their separate rooms and start their honeymoon aboard the ship.

After a quick breakfast, Mr. Bridges drove them all to the docks where the RMS Mauretania was berthed. Petra and Marek didn't know how to thank the Bridges enough. Mr. Bridges simply stated that it had been an honour for Ms. Bridges and himself to help a Czech hero and his wife 'in a small way.' The Bridges promised to make their long wished for visit to Prague next year, bringing Lucie with them, when they could all be together again.

Chapter Eighteen

After waving good-bye, Marek and Petra found their cabin. Not large but an adequate size, clean and tastefully decorated on a maritime theme, it would be a comfortable place for the
voyage of only six days. They then went on deck, joining almost all the passengers to watch as they sailed from America with a view of the tall buildings of Manhattan and the Statue of Liberty clearly visible in the background. They explored the shops, that is in the second class area. It was forbidden for them to wander around the first class deck but in the confusion of boarding they walked up a flight of stairs to see the opulent large atrium, with a huge staircase reserved for passengers travelling first class. The second class area was, to them, very pleasant. The décor was elegant and there were many sitting rooms, all with comfortable leather chairs, two dining rooms, a ballroom, a concert hall, a gymnasium, a room full of small tables on which were lots of board games, a hair dressing salon, a doctor's surgery, a nursery, a prayer room, and numerous shops.

In the cabin they found a folder of documents about the ship and the facilities. The RMS Mauretania was a sister ship to the RMS Lusitania, torpedoed by German submarines early in the war with a great loss of life, including neutral Americans. The present ship carried over two thousand passengers in the three classes and had a crew of eight hundred on the eight decks. For this voyage the ship was full in all classes due to the heavy demand for transatlantic voyages. There was even a daily ship's newspaper, containing a summary of world events and a description of the entertainment available to passengers.

Dinner was a rather formal affair, beginning at seven o'clock. There were many tables for eight people with name cards indicating where each person should sit. The first evening was taken up by introductions. A middle-aged Englishman introduced himself and his wife, explaining that they lived in Manchester and he had been in New York on business, without specifying what the nature of the business was. He turned to Marek.

'I see you are listed as Major Novak, retired, and Ms Novak. May I ask which army you served in?'

Marek explained briefly about the Czech and Slovak Legion. All at the table were fascinated, even if most of them did not quite grasp the context of the Legion which most of them had not heard of.

'So you were in the Russian army in the war and then you fought the Bolsheviks?' asked one lady.

Marek tried to clarify but the group became even more confused by what he admitted was a confusing story, so they passed on to other introductions. There was another British couple who strongly emphasised that they were Scottish, not English. They had been on holiday in Chicago, visiting her brother who had emigrated twenty five years ago. Then there were two single people. An American diplomat, taking up a position as Cultural Attaché in the London Embassy and a delicate looking Swedish lady who introduced herself in fluent English as an interior design architect. She and Petra had a lengthy talk about design. The British men argued rather heatedly about what they called 'the Irish problem.' Marek had difficulty following but he understood that it was a matter of granting independence to Ireland. He saw a similarity to his new country, Czechoslovakia. Why shouldn't the Irish be allowed to govern themselves? he wondered. Apparently there were religious problems concerning the Catholic church and a large group of protestants which

Marek did not understand. Nor could he understand what the position was of the parties in Westminster, so he said nothing.

After dinner Marek and Petra looked in to the dancing in the spacious ballroom as the band played what Petra recognised as a Fox Trot. Deciding to come back the following evening, they went to their cabin to spend their first night together.

During the next days, Marek and Petra enjoyed the facilities available on the ship. They looked in the shops at the delicate, expensive jewellery without spending any money. In the games room, Marek watched as two men played chess. When the game was over the winner challenged him to a game. They were fairly evenly matched but after an hour and about forty moves, the position became blocked and they agreed a draw.

On three evenings they went to the dance hall but only danced once. Marek was hampered by his useless left arm and, concluded Petra, he had what was referred to in the classes she had attended as a teenager as having 'two left feet!' On the other visits they simply enjoyed the music.

Petra recalled Bill's description of the dances and she recounted them to Marek. In recent years several 'animal trot' dances had become popular, such as the Fox Trot. There had been the Turkey Trot, where the dancers jumped about to fast rhythms making movements which some people considered to be offensively suggestive. Attempts were made to ban them. Being denounced by the Vatican only increased their popularity. Another violent dance was the Grizzly Bear, in which the dancers would shout together, 'I'm a Bear.' These faded in popularity and only the Fox Trot survived. It was a graceful dance in 4/4 time, not unlike the elegant waltz in 3/4 time.

Petra became concerned when, night after night, Marek would wake sitting up and shouting. They went to the doctor to seek advice.

'It is understandable after your terrible experiences and I have encountered it in many soldiers who fought in the trenches in France. In England we call it 'shell shock.' It will pass, but it may take months or even years. I could give you tablets but frankly I don't believe they do much good. Just try to get a lot of other happy experiences which will eventually black out the awful ones and try to adopt a hopeful outlook to the future. If it doesn't get better, see a specialist when you get home,' the doctor advised.

When Petra was resting one day, Marek was walking around the shop area when he noticed the office of the chaplain. Marek had had little connection with the Church since moving to Prague in his late teens but on the voyage from Vladivostok he looked back on his life over the last six years. 'Where was God at this time? He could do anything – what was the term? - omnipotent, he thought : then why had He allowed this mass killing?' Perhaps the chaplain could explain that to him. So he knocked on the door which was answered by a middle-aged man wearing a clerical collar.

'Please come in and have a cup of tea or coffee, and if you wish we can talk,' he greeted Marek in a very friendly tone.

'What has brought you to knock on my door?'

After accepting the cup of tea, Marek explained what he had been asking himself about God's absence - that is even if He exists, which he was doubting.

'Many people have been asking that question, just as I was doing in the years I spent in France with the British army. The way I have come to see it is this. When God created man he gave him free agency, freedom to do good or evil. God's alternative would have been to restrict him to thinking and doing only certain things, effectively creating man as a sort of puppet.'

'But if He can perform miracles why didn't He prevent or stop the killing,' Marek asked .

'Yes, God does occasionally perform miracles. We don't know how He does it, nor why He chooses to intervene in one situation and not in another. For example, to have prevented the killing in Russia He would have had to intervene in millions of lives over centuries of evil treatment of generations of serfs. Evil actions begin with evil thoughts. Where would millions of miracles have had to have begun? It would amount to taking away free agency from entire populations,' explained the chaplain.

They talked on for almost an hour about this and other subjects. Marek told him something of his early life in what had now become Czechoslovakia, his experiences in Russia, his recent marriage and his ambitions for the future. The chaplain explained that he too had had a difficult time in France and adjusting to peacetime activities had not been easy. He took this job with Cunard to serve people and to give himself a time to let the Lord heal his spirit. He was an ordained priest of the Church of England. Marek questioned him about the differences between his church and the Catholic church and he became very interested in the subject. Before leaving the chaplain asked if he may say a prayer for Marek and his wife. Marek agreed and the chaplain did so. He also recommended two books which would be available in German.

The voyage was nearly over. Dinner conversation had been lively every evening. Marek, as usual, had not been very talkative and he had several times declined to discuss his time in Russia. The British diners talked of politics which he didn't quite understand except that they were critical of their government. Petra talked with the Swedish lady and had several quite animated, good natured conversations with the American Cultural Attaché about his views on painting and music. They were both well informed on these subjects and enjoyed the exchange of anecdotes and opinions. They too kept clear of the war in their conversations. On the last evening they carried out the routine of exchanging addresses, hoping to meet again somewhere but really knowing that that would not happen.

Chapter Nineteen

Arriving early in the morning and disembarking at Southampton most of the passengers took the direct 'boat train' to London. Not wishing to spend time or money in England they found the next train from London to Dover and then a ferry for the four-hour crossing to Ostend in Belgium. Making enquiries for the next morning, they learned that there was an early train to Brussels which would connect after a three hour wait to another to Germany and then on to Prague, a two day journey. It was late, already dark for some hours, so the travellers found a cheap hotel near the station and had a good night's sleep before being wakened by the owner at six o'clock. They ate a quick breakfast of coffee and croissants and walked over to the railway station.

The train to Brussels was old, certainly pre-war and there were few passengers. From the window Marek and Petra saw scenes of devastation in Flanders, villages and railway stations virtually destroyed. The war had ended two years ago and there were signs of renewal among the ruins.

They changed trains in Brussels, bought a snack of food in a paper package and took another Belgian train to the German border. They had a long argument with the German border police because they hadn't got the correct documents. Eventually a more senior officer was called who looked through their papers, listened to their explanations and let them through. Another tedious journey to Munich and a night there in a hotel before taking yet another train to the border of Czechoslovakia.

The attitude of the Czech border police could not have been more different. After hearing an outline of their stories, the policemen stretched out their arms in welcome. Marek held back tears but Petra couldn't. An officer took them over to the train bound for Prague. They were home at last!

They had sent a short telegram from London via Bata saying that they would soon arrive but not on which day so there was no one to meet them. They decided to visit Petra's parents in Prague before going on to Zlin. Laughter filled the hall and tears flowed as they walked into the house.

'This is my new husband, Marek Novak,' said Petra, introducing him to her mother and father. Although surprised, they accepted Marek immediately (they knew of Filip's death). It was evening, they couldn't rush away, so they stayed overnight. The parents wanted to hear their stories and to tell theirs. They had survived the war and the following famine. Now things were better, shops had goods to sell, people were getting jobs. The parents approved of President Masaryk's government which was working hard to bring life in the country back to normal. Petra's father was back at his old job as curator of the big city art gallery. It had been closed during the war and the most valuable paintings had been stored for safety deep in a wine cellar in the country. Before leaving for Zlin the following morning they went to a neighbour's office where there was a telephone and got through to Tomas Bata. He was delighted to hear Marek's voice. Marek asked about the business.

'We expanded and made a lot of money making boots in the war. Changing back to shoes has been difficult. People have little money and there are still food shortages. The large work force has to be retrained and I have tried to keep them well, with free meals and medical attention, but our finances are again very tight.'

Bata promised to send a message immediately to his parents to tell them when the train would arrive.

They were all there on the station platform, his parents Pavel and Veronika and numerous neighbours. Just as with Petra's parents, there were scenes of laughter and tears of joy. They had had no time to prepare a welcome feast, but now set about doing so. The lunch celebrations went on to run into supper.

Tomas Bata was happy to allow his telephone to be used. Next day Marek got through to the President's office and asked for an appointment with the President.

'I'm afraid that the President is very busy,' said the gate-keeper. After some explanations and particularly the fact that Marek had met President Masaryk in Russia during the war, the official relented.

'I can give you a slot on Tuesday next at three o'clock, just before the cabinet meeting,' he said.

'I'll be there.'

Next in line for the telephone was Veronika to let her mother know that her grandson and his wife would come to see her the next day around lunch time. The elderly lady was happy. She had been lonely after her husband died two years ago after a long illness and a depression caused by the closure of the family's glassworks.

So next day, Petra, Marek and his mother went to see the elderly lady. She was overwhelmed with joy to see her grandson again and to meet his wife.

'Where did you meet? Where did you marry? In which church, Catholic or Protestant?' she wanted to know. With some embarrassment Marek had to admit that they had not had a church ceremony.

'That is shocking! A civil wedding, and in America of all places, that is not a proper marriage. You must go through a real ceremony in a Catholic church and stop living in sin. I will speak with our parish priest and he can arrange it. In the meantime you must sleep in separate rooms because you are not properly married!' Granny was not going to give in so easily. There seemed to be nothing to do but accept the inevitable and anyway it would be easier to live in Czechoslovakia with a valid local marriage certificate rather than the American one which they held. It was agreed that the wedding would take place as soon as possible in her parish church. On the way home the three all chuckled about Granny's reaction. If that was what she wanted, they would comply.

Later that evening Marek thought back to his talk with the chaplain on the ship. He had been baptised as a Catholic but his attendance at Church had reduced to attending mass at Christmas and Easter. There were aspects of the Church's teaching and practices which he couldn't accept but he didn't wish to cut himself off, so a Church wedding would at least keep his membership 'in order.' He wondered – if he didn't believe certain things then what did he believe ? He determined to pursue this question. He had clear career ambitions but were they enough ?

On Tuesday morning Marek visited the office of the Legion. The staff there were helping Legionnaires to settle back into life in commerce, industry, in government service, in the army and on their farms. He was told that from the admittedly incomplete lists over sixty thousand had boarded ships in Vladivostok. A few had stayed in America or Canada. The list of dead and missing was certainly incomplete since the number of stragglers who didn't reach the coast was not known – and probably never would be. Including those who had died in battle the total could exceed the number who got home. Marek asked whether they could give him the address of Stefan's parents or other members of his family. The staff member promised to find the addresses and asked him to come back the following week.

On his walk through the city Marek passed what had once been his favourite coffee house and his university. He made a mental note to call in to enquire about his degree. He had taken the exams in June 1914, only weeks before the outbreak of war. Had his final exams been graded?, he wondered. And what had happened to the professors? Some would have been of military age: had they survived the war?

Marek was in the President's office before three o'clock. He was asked to wait. After half an hour President Masaryk was free.

'Welcome back!' he said greeting Marek cordially. 'Life has changed since we last met in Omsk. You are looking well.'

Not quite true but a lot better than you are, thought Marek. He was now seventy and showing the strains of his office.

'What do you intend to do now that you are back,' he enquired.

'I wish to serve you in establishing a country that we can be proud of in the coming years,' Marek stated.

'Excellent. You held the rank of major in the Legion. We need experienced officers in our army and you could retain the rank,' he proposed. 'We have border clashes with Hungary and Poland and I have had to commit our small army to the defence of the country.'

'Thank you, Sir, but I have had enough of violence and killing to last me for a lifetime. I would like to join the diplomatic service. I have studied economics, law and politics and I speak English and Russian quite well,' replied Marek. 'My wife speaks French and I could learn it quickly.'

The President thought for a minute, which seemed more like an hour to Marek. 'If that is what you really want, and it seems to me that it is, I will arrange it with the Foreign Minister. In fact, he will be here for a meeting at five o'clock, so if you can be here again at quarter to five, we can arrange everything.'

When he returned the Foreign Minister was with the President. He had already explained who Marek was and what he wanted.

'We would be glad to have you on our team,' said the Minister. 'Please come to my building on Monday morning and ask for the Chief of Personnel. He will arrange the terms of your employment. I'm sure that you will serve with distinction.'

Marek thanked them both and walked out to meet Petra who had been waiting patiently in a coffee house. He had a big smile on his face. He would achieve his lifetime ambition.

'I will work for a free and independent Czechoslovakia.'

*

'A single death is a tragedy. A million deaths is a statistic.'
Josef Stalin